ENTICED BY A KINGPIN

BOOK 1

MIA BLACK

CHAPTER 1

"Good morning, Dr. Jameson," said Tommy, the doorman of my building as I stepped out of the elevator and into the lobby. I only had one headphone in as I walked over to the desk where he was seated.

Tommy was an older Italian and Hispanic man who'd worked at the building for years, much longer than I'd been living there. He was sweet and kind; always having a conversation for those who were willing to stop and hear it.

"Good morning Tommy," I said with a smile. "I told you before that you can call me Kallie. All that doctor stuff is for the hospital."

"You work too hard for people not to call you by your title," he said with a kind smile. "Headed out for your morning run?"

I nodded my head. "You know it," I said as I headed towards the door. "I'll see you in a little bit."

"Have fun. It's beautiful out today," he said.

I stepped out of the building and onto the bright streets of my Chicago neighborhood. Tommy wasn't lying, it was beautiful out. There were a couple of clouds in the sky but the sun was shining brightly and warming my skin up. I put my headphones in and tucked my phone into my armband and started my run.

I loved my area because even though the street that I lived on had a few tall apartment buildings, there was a park with beautiful running trails inside of it not too far away. As I headed towards the park, I saw the same people that I saw mostly every day. I tried to run at the same time daily whenever it could be helped. It looked like something out of a movie with the trendy coffee shops, tall trees, and white people out walking their dogs. I paid an arm and a leg to live there but it was more than worth it.

I still lived in the same city that I grew up in

but it didn't feel like it sometimes. People heard on the news about how rough it was to grow up on the Southside of Chicago but actually being there was something else. We heard gunshots all the time and gangs were always around. We didn't live in fear but we knew better than to be out after the street lights came on. Don't get me wrong, though, I loved my city, which was why I hadn't left.

From a young age I knew I wanted to be a doctor. It was more than just watching medical shows and falling in love with them. I wanted to help people. I wanted to be a healer. Most of all, I wanted to be able to give back and help out those who needed it.

I was in the process of finishing my residency at Summit Hospital. Getting to my residency had been a process in and of itself. I got good grades in school and qualified for scholarships but financially speaking, I'd only made it through medical school by the skin of my teeth. I was glad to be finally finishing up my training so that I could become a full-fledged doctor.

I ran through the park and enjoyed the early morning weather. While on one of my favorite trails, I ran into a handsome white guy who made sure that I noticed him looking up and down my body as he ran passed me. I just kept it moving without trying to make too much eye contact. I was on a schedule and didn't want to stop, especially since he was probably just gonna try and spit some game at me.

Being 25 years old, most people underestimated me, especially in the medical field. I'd had to prove myself over and over again because when people looked at me, all they saw was a pretty face with a nice body. Standing at 5'4", I had the figure of an athlete but not as muscled up. My thick thighs, perfectly round ass, and small but nice hips had always gotten the attention of guys. Pair that up with my smooth, pecan colored skin, thick, wavy hair that came just to my shoulders, and almond shaped gray eyes and you had a bombshell. I was pretty, but I had to let people know that I'd gotten to where I was because of my brains, not my beauty.

I finished my run and headed back to my condo to shower and change. I'd worked up quite and sweat and was ready to clean all the dirt off of me. I wasn't scheduled to work that day, but I was on call. It meant that if my hospital issued pager went off, I needed to get to work. I had a couple of on call days each week and only one had gone by without my being paged so I was ready for it. Like clockwork, I heard the familiar beep of the pager letting me know that I needed to head in.

I got dressed, throwing on a pair of black dress pants and a simple white shirt. My doctors' coat was at work in my locker. I kept a duffle bag packed and ready to go all the time in case I needed to head in at a moment's notice. We worked long shifts and could sometimes be at the hospital for an entire day without heading home once so I made sure the duffle was always packed with essentials: another outfit, deodorant, phone charger, and more.

"Headed out again so soon?" Tommy asked as I stepped back into the lobby. I'd ordered an Uber and it was outside waiting for me.

"Yep," I said with a nod. "Duty calls."

"Go save some lives," Tommy said. He said the same thing to me every time I left the building and headed to the hospital.

"I'll try," I said with a smile as I stepped out of the building.

Summit Hospital was a huge building with

several smaller buildings all around it that they also owned. I'd been working there for the last two years and had seen a lot of people come and go, not just doctors or nurses either.

The hospital was one of the busiest in the city. We had a first-class triage center in the E.R. which meant that we were equipped to deal with all types of cases and I'd seen my fair share of things while working at the hospital.

Being so focused on my career meant that I didn't really have time for other things but I was alright with that. My schedule kept me more than busy. On a daily basis I could be found all over the hospital depending on the need. As a resident, I needed to be able to see every side of the medical field and what it had to bring. I'd been in the Emergency Room as well as in the Intensive Care Unit. I went where there was a need for me.

I stepped out of my Uber and headed inside the hospital. I knew all of the people who worked there and it was always nice to see them, even when bad things were happening. I checked in with my attending doctor and headed straight to work.

Clinic Duty was a bitch and everyone tried

to avoid it as much as possible. I, on the other hand, loved it. It gave me a chance to work directly with the community and see more people who had less complicated issues.

I headed downstairs to our clinic and got to work seeing patients. My morning was busy as hell, running through person after person. A lot of them were just follow ups from the E.R. which made it easy to get through them. It could become very routine at time because a lot of it was just the same things that every doctor did: breathing checks, blood pressure, and taking blood before sending you on your merry way. I liked the cases that were outside of the ordinary because they made everything more exciting. Along with that excitement came the fact that sometimes I had to give people bad news.

Things finally calmed down for me shortly before lunch time. Even lunch was a privilege when you worked in a hospital; you never knew what patients might need your attention and would keep you working. Thankfully Clinic Duty was pretty much a straight shot which freed me up to head to lunch. I just needed to find Stella since we'd made plans to go out together.

Stella Frasier was my closest friend sincere medical school and she also happened to be my attending doctor. Stella was finishing up just as I was coming into the college. We met because the school had a program that paired someone who was leaving up with someone who was just starting. It was one of those mentor and mentee situations.

Stella and I clicked immediately. It might have been because we were among the small handful of Black women enrolled in the program, or because of our love for what we did. Either way, she was my homegirl. After she graduated we kept in touch and it was a no-brainer than I'd end up at the same hospital that she worked at. I loved working under her because she cared about what she did.

Stella and I didn't have the same back-ground. She came from a close knit, well to do family. They were well known around the city and had been for years, thanks to their money and power. She never tried to act grand though. In fact, she wanted her work to speak for itself and never tried to use her last name for clout.

I headed downstairs to the Nurse's Station in the Emergency Room. Stella *loved* working in the E.R. She said that she lived a pretty regular life growing up and seeing the trauma and excitement of the E.R. was exhilarating to her. I told her she sounded like an adrenaline junky sometimes but she always just laughed it off.

Stella was finishing up a conversation with a nurse when I saw her. I stood off to the side and waited for the conversation to finish before I made my way over.

"Hey, how was the clinic?" Stella asked with a smile. Stella towered over me normally but she was wearing heels that day so she was extra tall.

"It was exactly what you'd expect it to be," I said. "I had to admit this one guy though. Poor thing."

"Why? What happened?" She asked. Stella liked to be informed of things so I tried to keep communication between us open. We hadn't run into any issues with her supervising me yet and I didn't want to start.

I shook my head. "This guy comes in for a follow-up because he was here two weeks ago for liver issues. We prescribed him some pills," I said.

"And let me guess, he didn't take them?" she asked.

"No, he took 'em," I said. "He just drank beer with every damn pill. His liver is probably shot. They're running some tests on him now."

Stella shook her head. "If only they'd listen to us," she said grimly. "How are you otherwise?"

"I'm good. I'm hungry as hell though," I said. "I went for a run this morning and didn't get a chance to eat a whole meal."

"I know how that is," Stella said. She stepped a little closer to me so no one would hear her and then smirked. "Jay left my house this morning and then I got paged to come in."

I scoffed and playfully rolled my eyes. "Oh gosh. Who is Jay?" Stella was 30 years old but didn't look like she was past her mid-twenties. She was 5'9" with brown skin and light blonde and brown curly hair. Stella was *always* on point. Her outfits were always nice and her coat was never dirty. She carried herself with confidence and grace.

"I'll tell you over lunch," she said with a grin on her face. "But, we have to push lunch back a little bit."

"Ugh, why?" I asked.

"Girl you know I'm trying to get that promotion," she said. "I can't do it unless people know who I am."

"But everyone knows who you are, Stella," I said.

"Not the right people," she said. "If I wanna move up, I need to get some face time with the Board members. That's why I volunteered to be a part of the fundraising committee. People know I'm good at what I do but I need them to see me as more than that."

Stella was incredible ambitious and never tried to make excuses for it. She wasn't cutthroat or anything like that but she made it known that she had goals that she wanted to meet for herself. "When's the meeting?" I asked.

"It starts in a few minutes," she said as she looked down at her watch.

"Alright, I'll just go with you then if that's cool. Otherwise we might not make it to lunch," I said.

"Come on then, let's go," she said.

Stella and I made our way up to the seventh-floor conference room where the meeting was taking place. I'd only been to one or two board meetings since I'd been at the hospital. Honestly, I was only there was for the patients. The politics of the hospital were for other people to worry about, not me.

I walked into the large room right after Stella. The hug windows had a beautiful view of the city that could be seen from most of the hospital. I looked at the front of the room and saw the place where the board members were seated. They were all the usual people that you'd imagine were on a board for a hospital, all of them except for Christian Harper. I'd seen him around the hospital in passing but he and I locked eyes for a brief moment and I felt like he was looking at me.

Christian Harper stood out from the rest of the board members because he was the only Black person on the board, and the youngest as well. Christian was 34 years old and came from a wealthy family. More importantly, he was a big player in the pharmaceutical world which is where he earned his money. He'd given a lot of money to the hospital and had helped them secure a couple of big medicine deals over the years which had earned him his spot on the board.

Christian had a reputation around the hospital for being a player. From what I'd heard, he'd been through his fair share of the female doctors and nurses. I'd really only seen him in passing but I couldn't lie and say he wasn't nice to look at. He was 6'2" with light brown skin and short curly hair. He looked like he worked out and kept himself in shape, but he didn't look 34 at all. Word around the hospital was that he was arrogant, but I'd heard from some people that it was just because he was confident. I mean, if you were rich and powerful and knew it, you'd probably come across a little arrogant too.

The meeting didn't take too long. I didn't know how many meetings they'd had before this but they just went over a couple of quick ideas. I only halfway paid attention. I was more focused on getting out to eat so I could come back and do my rounds.

When the meeting was over, Stella and I stood up to leave. We were making small talk about where we wanted to eat when someone called out to Stella.

"Dr. Frasier?" a deep male voice said from behind us. We stopped walking and turned around to see Christian making his way up to us. He was walking quickly but there was a smoothness about it that didn't make it seem like he was in a rush.

"Hello Mr. Harper," she said. "How are you?"

"I'm doing well," he said. "How are you?" Before Stella could answer, his brown eyes shifted from Stella to me. "And you must be Dr. Jameson, am I right?"

I felt my face get warm as I took his hand in mine to shake it. "Have we met? I'm sorry if I don't remember," I said, feeling slightly embarrassed.

He shook his head and smiled with a set of perfect white teeth. "I'm sorry about that. No, we haven't met. I just make it my business to know who's doing well and who's not and I've heard nothing but good things about you. I hear you have a real passion for your patients."

I smiled, feeling flattered. "Thank you. I love what I do," I said.

"No problem at all," he said. "You remind me a lot of myself." He looked down at his watch and then pulled his phone out of his pocket. "I'm sorry but I have to run," he said as he reached down into his pocket, pulled out a business card and handed it to me, "but you can take my card and give me a call in case you ever want to get away from the hospital."

Before I could say anything, he said goodbye and exited the room. I looked up at Stella, who's eyebrows were about to touch her hairline cause they were so damn high. "Alright then," she said with a smirk and then burst out laughing.

Stella and I left the hospital and made our way to the restaurant that we'd decided to go to. It was a beautiful day outside and I hoped that we could find seats somewhere outdoors to enjoy the weather.

"So, are you gonna give Christian a call?" Stella asked as we walked.

"I don't know, Stella," I admitted.

"Oh gosh," she said. "Don't start that up again. You need to live a little. Just give him a call."

"He's handsome and everything but I don't know about it," I said. "I'm just really focused on my career right now."

Stella stopped walking where we were and folded her arms across her chest. "Kallie, you've been doing that same song and dance since we

met one another back in med school. I understand being focused but you know that if you
stare at something for too long then it goes out
of focus," Stella said.

I grabbed her by the arm playfully to get her
to keep moving. "Alright, I'm listening," I said.

"There's nothing wrong with being focused
but you gotta live a little too," she said. "You've
been pushing yourself for years and I think you
forget sometimes that you've made it. No more
grades, you're a doctor now. You deserve to take
a little break and enjoy yourself and Christian
may be just what you need."

"You have a point," I admitted.

"I know I do," she joked. "Speaking of
points, when was the last time you got some?"

I screwed my face up at her. "Girl, you know
I don't talk about that," I said.

"Damn, that long, huh? You used to tell me
about it, but it's been a while. I'd swear you were
a virgin if I didn't know any better."

"Haha, real funny," I said. "I'm not out here
jumping from person to person like you are but
I'm fine."

"Don't knock it till you try it," Stella said. "I
live my life just fine."

Stella liked moving from guy to guy. It was kind of her thing. I think that deep down she wanted to find someone to be with but she was having fun until she found him. I couldn't knock her though because as she said, she lived her life just fine.

When we got to the restaurant, Stella kept on going with her crusade to get me to go out with Christian or at least give him a call.

"He's clearly into you," Stella said. "He and I only speak in the hallway if we happen to bump into one another, but he made a beeline for you me as soon as he saw you."

"I'll think about it," I finally said. I didn't want to become annoyed with Stella because she was only trying to look out for me but it was getting to be a little pushy on her part. "That's the best that I can do."

"Alright," Stella said. It seemed like she was picking up on my attitude so she changed the topic.

Stella and I enjoyed our lunch and took a long and slow walk back to the hospital to enjoy the fresh air. The rest of the afternoon went by quickly and I lucked out by not having to stay later than I was scheduled.

When I got home I followed up my usual routine. I cooked myself some dinner; salmon and mashed potatoes. I grabbed my plate and plopped down in front of the TV with a bottle of wine.

I knew that Stella was only trying to help me out earlier. What she was saying was true; it had been a while since I'd been out with anyone or even had sex but I had my reasons for not wanting to put myself out there and take the risk.

Life for me had been far from easy and though I hadn't left my city, I told myself that I wanted to leave my old life behind and I did. Small things could mean the biggest risk for someone growing up in Chicago like I did. If you didn't know the right people, or if you knew the wrong ones, it all could put your life at risk.

Since I got up out of the hood I hadn't looked back. I didn't like the life of looking over my shoulder or knowing how quickly I might have to jump into the bathtub to avoid gunfire. I guess that growing up that way and then leaving it behind made me afraid of taking risks.

I saw going out with Christian as a risk. I'd worked hard to create my own little corner of the world and it had everything that I wanted. I also had a schedule and had managed to live my life drama free. I intended on keeping it that way and going out with Christian might have messed it all up for me. I planned on keeping it that way, at least for now.

CHAPTER 2

A week later I was at the hospital working an early shift. I'd been there since before the sun came up and it was almost 11 in the morning. My schedule was always packed so I didn't even get enough sleep the night before. I pushed through though and made me rounds.

I was on call for the next few hours so after I finished up with my last patient, I decided to take a nap. It wouldn't be worth it to go all the way back home just to have to come right back out. Hospitals had on call rooms where doctors and nurses could sleep and refresh themselves between shifts. The bunk beds weren't the most comfortable thing in the world but most of us were usually so tired that it didn't really make a difference.

I was headed down the hallway towards the elevators when I spotted Christian. It looked like he was coming out of a meeting or something because he was shaking hands and smiling at people as they exited the room. I still hadn't called him and thankfully Stella hadn't asked about it so I hadn't really thought about it.

I would have just kept walking towards the elevator but he turned around and spotted me. He kept on shaking hands but kept his eyes trained on me. When I finally got to where he was, he waved me down and stopped me, pulling me to the side of the hall opposite the nurse's station.

"Hey Dr. Jameson, can I talk to you really quickly?" Christian's deep voice said.

"Sure, what's up?" I asked. I stared into his eyes.

"You know, usually when I give someone my number, they call," he said in an arrogant tone. I was looking at his face and the expression hadn't changed, letting me know just how serious he was. I figured that he wasn't used to women turning him down or not falling as his feet when he walked into a room. He had a lot going for himself but it was gonna take a whole lot more to impress me.

He was still a board member and it was already inappropriate enough that we were flirting so I decided to be honest but not hurtful. He needed to be checked and that meant that I might end up hurting his ego a little bit. It was fine because it seemed like he needed to be brought down a peg or two from his high horse.

"Honestly, Christian, I'm just not interested in dating," I said. I made sure my voice was firm as I spoke to him. I wanted him to know how serious I was.

His jaw clenched a little but when he spoke he sounded calm. "And why is that?" He asked.

"Work takes up all of my time," I said. "Actually, I'm on my way up to the on-call room to take a nap right now. I just don't have the time to see anyone. I hope you're not offended."

"I'm *never* offended," he said quickly. "Well, you still have my card, so if you change your mind, give me a call."

I opened my mouth to speak but someone called my name. "Dr. Jameson, do you have a minute? I have a question about one of your patients."

I looked passed Christian to see Dr. Ashley Ferrara calling out to me. Ashley was one of the attending doctors, same as Stella. She was a petite Latina woman with a small but curvy frame. I'd worked with Ashley a couple of times and I knew that she and Stella were only cordial. The two were constantly in competition because they were ambitious.

Ashley walked over to us. "Sorry about this Mr. Harper, but I need Kalie here for a moment," she said as she grabbed my arm, clearly not about to take no for an answer.

"No problem. I was just heading out anyways," he said before he nodded his head at us and walked away.

Ashley pulled me into the empty room that was opposite the nurses' station. I looked at her hands and she didn't have any charts with her. I also couldn't think of any patients that we were treating in common, so I didn't know what it was about.

"Sorry about that," she said, "but I saw you were in trouble and I wanted to help you out."

A look of confusion crossed my face. "Trouble? What do you mean?" I knew I might have looked a little uncomfortable but I hoped I wasn't giving off the impression that he was being unprofessional or anything.

"Christian...I mean Mr. Harper," she said. The look on her face was one of pure concern but there was something else there that I was starting to think was jealousy.

"What about him?" I asked. I wasn't about to offer up any information in case she got the wrong impression from seeing us talk.

"You should stay away from him. He has a reputation...if you catch my drift," she said. Ashley could be a lot at times from what I'd seen and I was seeing some of the crazy Latina chick stuff that I'd heard about.

"What kind of reputation?" I asked her. I wanted her to give me more information.

"*You know,*" she said with a look of annoyance on her face. "He's jumped in and out of the beds of a lot of people in the hospital. I just don't want to see that happen to you." She paused dramatically, putting her hand on her hip and then looking down at the floor while shaking her head. "Honestly, I was dumb enough to fall for his stuff too. He took me out a couple of times and wined and dined me. But after we slept together, it was a different story. I just don't wanna see that happen to you."

I didn't know how sincere she was being but she was an attending doctor so admitting something like that could get her into trouble. I figured I could trust her a little bit. "Thanks for the concern but I'm not interested in him," I said. She seemed to relax a little bit then. "That was actually what I was just telling him."

Ashley got a smile on her face. "Smart girl," she said. "Well, I'll let you be on your way."

I took my nap upstairs and was pleasantly surprised when I woke up to see that they wouldn't need me at work that night. Stella and I decided to go and get dinner since we hadn't really seen each other during the week. I also wanted to tell her about my conversation with Ashley, so it worked out.

I told Stella everything that happened with Christian and Ashley as we ate. She frowned when I told her what I told Christian about not being interested. When I got to the part about Ashley, she rolled her eyes a bunch of times.

"Well the stuff about Christian is true," she confirmed for me. I was a little taken aback by it. I'd heard the rumors but hearing Stella tell me they were true was something else.

"Really? How do you know?" I asked.

"It doesn't take a rocket scientist to figure it out," she said. "A man that good looking, still single, and working around all these hot in the pants doctors and nurses? I've heard stories about him."

"What kind of stories?" I asked.

"The kind that make me sure that you should give him a call," she said with a smirk. "I heard that he knows all the nicest places to go and that the sex is off the chain."

I screwed my face up at her. "Damn, they talking about him like that?"

She nodded her head. "Yeah, I've heard the same thing from a couple of people," she said. "I know you're trying to stay drama free or whatever but that's exactly why he might be right for you. From what I can gather, he's not looking for anything serious and neither are you. You can just go out on a couple of dates and get some good dick."

I burst out laughing. If our patients could hear the way we talk about stuff sometimes, they'd probably me mortified. They think we're all prim and proper. "I can't with you," I said. "But what about all that Ashley stuff. Is that true too?"

Stella rolled her eyes again. "Yeah, I heard about that too. But what she told you and what I heard are two different stories."

I leaned in a little bit and took a sip of my wine. "Spill," I said.

"From what people said, they chilled out a couple of times and went on a few dates. But she got a little obsessive and he dumped her ass like a bad habit."

I nodded my head like I'd been there myself when all of that happened. "You know, I got that vibe from her. She was normal all the other times I'd seen her but she turned it into a big thing to stop me from talking to him. You think she's jealous?"

"Probably," she said with a nod. "I'm sure if you ask around you'll probably hear about other people having similar conversations with Ashley. That's why he ended it with her in the first place."

"Damn girl, you're just spilling all the tea tonight," I said. "You know I stay out of the hospital drama so I didn't know any of this."

"That's what I'm here for," Stella said.

"I would have never picked Ashley to be the crazy type though," I said. "But I guess we don't really know one another outside of the hospital so she could really be anything."

"Yeah, that's true," Stella said. "But forget about her. What about you and Christian?"

"I still don't know, Stella," I admitted. "I mean, should I be concerned about him being a board member?"

"I get what you're saying, but he has just as much to lose as you do. It won't get out," she said. "But it's on you. I'm just trying to help you out."

"And I appreciate it," I said.

Stella and I finished up dinner a little bit later and I headed back to my condo. I unlocked the door and stepped inside. I turned on the light, illuminating the entire room and showcasing the beautiful view from my window.

Have you ever looked at something that was supposed to make you happy and instead you felt sad? That was how I felt as I made my way over to my couch. I didn't know if it was Stella's rambling about getting out or what, but I suddenly realized that for all my talk about routine, my life had become boring. I went out with Stella every now and then but even that was usually just a dinner or drinks somewhere. I got up, ran, and went to work pretty much every day. It was becoming boring.

I realized how much time I *hadn't* been spending actually living. I was dedicated to my work and to my patients but at times it almost felt like a thankless job. I realized how little time I'd spent doing the things that I enjoyed. I hadn't even really been out to enjoy all the new spots to go to in my neighborhood and I'd lived there for over two years.

I didn't know if he would be a cure or a quick fix but the more I sat there thinking about it, the more I realized that Christian might just be the thing I need to add some excitement to my life. I went to my purse and grabbed his card. I headed back over to the couch and plopped back down on it with my phone in my hand.

"No time like the present," I said out loud. I only had one glass of wine at the restaurant with Stella so it wasn't like my judgement was impaired. I knew what I was doing. I dialed the number from his business card. I didn't know if it was his cell or what but after a few seconds it started to ring.

"Hello?" Christian answered. "Christian Harper."

"Hello?" I nervously cleared my throat. It had been awhile since I'd spoken to someone I was attracted to on the phone. "Hey Christian. It's Dr. Jameson...Kallie. I decided to give you a call. I hope it's not too late."

"Kallie, it's nice to hear your voice," he said. "How are you?"

"I'm doing well, and yourself?" I asked.

"I'm good. I just got back in from the gym not too long ago," he said.

"Really? This late?"

He chuckled. "I gotta stay in shape," he said.

"I understand. I run every day," I said.

"I can see that," he said in a flirtatious tone. "So, I was thinking we should go and get drinks somewhere. I'd like to see you outside of the hospital setting. How about this weekend?"

Well, no one could ever say that Christian Harper was a man who didn't know what he wanted. He was definitely straight to the point. Something about him being so direct made me want to be the same. "This weekend is no good for me," I lied, "but what are you doing for the rest of the night?"

I could practically hear him smile through the phone. "I have no plans other than taking a shower. Why? What'd you have in mind?"

"How about we go grab a drink some-where?" I asked. I knew he was probably hoping that I was gonna invite him to my house but even though I was being adventurous, I didn't want him to get any ideas.

"That sounds good. Did you have a place? If not, I know of somewhere that we can," he said.

"That sounds good. Wanna meet up in an hour? If you text me address, I'll take a cab and meet you there," I said.

"I'm nothing if not a gentleman," he said. "Text me your address and I'll come and pick you up. It's the least I can do since you called me."

Christian was charming, that was for sure. "Alright," I said. "I'll be ready in about 30 minutes."

"See you then," he said before getting off the phone.

I hopped in the shower to wash the day off of me. I didn't have a lot of time to get ready so I planned what I was wearing while in the shower. I had a lot of nice dresses that I didn't ever really get the chance to wear so it was about time that I finally got a chance to wear them.

I had this green cocktail dress that was cinched at the waist and showed off my cleavage. I out on a pair of black heels and ran a comb through my hair to give it more volume. I checked myself in the mirror and had to admit that I looked pretty good.

My phone started to ring right on time. It was Christian letting me know that he was downstairs. I grabbed my clutch and headed downstairs where I was greeted by the sight of him standing outside of a jet-black BMW.

We made our way to the lounge that he'd picked out. We made small talk all the way to the place and when we got inside, Christian got us a table for two. I looked around the lounge and I had to admit that I was impressed. It was a lot more upscale than some of the places that I'd been to. Christian must have come there often because he seemed to know a few people.

"What do you think of this place?" Christian asked as we looked around.

"The vibe is nice," I said as I took in the jazz music playing in the background. The crowd was very mixed. There seemed to be people from my age to people older than Christian. I could also tell that the people in here all had money. It was something I learned to pick up on while working at the hospital.

"Yeah, it is. It's a nice place to just come and have a few drinks. Do you know what you want?" he asked.

"Yeah. Can I have vodka and cranberry with lime?" I said. He nodded at me before waving a waiter down to get a drink.

While waiting for the drinks, I noticed that Christian's phone kept lighting up. It happened every few minutes and I tried not to look down at it too much but the light kept breaking up the conversation. He'd been doing his best to ignore it but he finally flipped it over to try and stop noticing it.

"I was surprised that you called me," Christian said. "After the way you told me you weren't interested earlier, I didn't think I'd hear from you. What changed your mind?"

"I had a conversation with myself," I said. The waiter came back and set the drinks down on the table. I squeezed one of the two slices of lime into the drink and took a sip. It tasted just the way I liked it.

"What kind of conversation?" he asked.

I opened my mouth to speak but I noticed the vibrations of the phone kept making buzzing noises on the table. "Are you gonna get that?" I asked. "It could be important."

"It's fine. I'm sure it's no one," he said.

I took another sip of my drink. "Are you sure it's not one of the women from the hospital? I heard about your reputation," I said. His phone had been going off for the last few minutes and since it was so late, I knew it couldn't have been work related. The only person or people that would call that much at this time of night would be a woman looking for a man.

If Christian was phased by me calling him out, he didn't show it. He took a tip of the whiskey and ginger ale that he'd ordered and then put it back down on the table. "Like I said, no one important," he said. He smirked at me.

"So, what's the gossip around the hospital about me?"

"Well, I've heard that you've been with a few people, including Ashley," I said. I wasn't about to back down since I was the one who'd brought it up.

"It's true that I've dipped in and out of one or two staff members of, but I'm sure it's not the way that you've heard" he admitted. "I make no excuses for it either. I'm a bachelor. I'm a self-made man. I'm not looking for a commitment right now and I make that clear to every woman that I deal with."

"That's really bold of you," I said.

He looked a little confused. "Really? I don't think so. I've found that in life, you have to speak your intentions clearly in order for people to take you seriously. I'm not looking to settle down yet. But I wouldn't mind finding someone who understands that I'm just looking for a non-complicated good time." He eyed me with lust in his eyes as he waited for my response.

"I understand that," I said. "I'm not looking for a commitment right now either. Like I said to you earlier, work comes first."

"See, nothing bold about it. You're just a

woman who knows what she does and doesn't want," he said.

I nodded my head. "I think we understand each other," I said. "But I wanna make one thing clear: I'm not trying to rush into anything."

"That's fine," he said. "The ball is in your court."

Christian and I had a few more drinks and got to know one another better. He was a very intelligent man and explained some of what he did in pharmaceutical sales. I told him more about why I became a doctor and where I hoped to take my career to. It seemed like we were building the beginnings of a friendship. We even toasted to it before we headed back to his car for him to drive me home.

When we pulled up outside of my building, Christian put the car into park and sat.

"Did you have a good time?" he asked. His handsome face kept being lit up by passing cars.

"I did," I admitted. Christian had been a complete gentleman the entire time. "What about you?"

"The same," he smiled. "I'm glad you called."

"Me too," I said. I put my hand on the door. "Well, I'll see you at the hospital."

"Can I walk you upstairs?" he asked.

I had no intentions on sleeping with Christian that night and I didn't want him to think that I was going to. I really did have a good time with him but it was still too soon. Now that we'd gone out, he'd given me a lot more to think about and I wanted to process it all...without sex clouding my judgement.

"It's alright," I said. "I have a doorman and stuff."

He looked a little disappointed but recovered quickly. Alright then, I'll give you a call soon," he said. He leaned in and pecked me on the lips quickly before I realized it. His lips were soft.

"Goodnight," I said.

"Night," he responded. He sat there until I went into my building.

CHAPTER 3

Early in the afternoon the following day I was making my rounds. It had been a busy morning. A child came in with the flu, which was completely out of season, so we had to separate him from everyone else before he started to spread it. It was a bit of a headache.

As I walked down the hall towards a nurse's station to get the charts for my next patient, I spotted Stella. She was coming out of one of the administrator's office. She smiled at me and walked over to me.

"Hey, what's got you so excited?" I asked. My eyes got wide. "Did you get the promotion?"

She kept the smile on her face but nodded

her head no. "Not yet, but I think I'm close," she said.

"Walk with me to my next patient," I said. "So, what happened?" I grabbed the chart and started to walk down the long hallway.

"Well, Dr. Hill just showered me with compliments. He says that he likes the way that I run the team and that he could really see me taking over the E.R. for real. He thinks I'd be a great fit."

"I'm happy for you!" I said. Stella had been working hard to move up so I knew the compliments meant a lot to her.

"Thanks," she said. "I don't have it yet but this makes me feel like it's only a matter of time. What's going on with you?"

"Well," I said with a smirk on my face, "I went out last night for drinks with Christian."

"Are you serious?" Stella asked in shock. "That's really good! It's about time you got out the house. How did it go?"

"Really well, actually," I said. "He was a gentleman."

"That's good and all, but did you guys...*you know*?" she asked as she nudged my shoulder a little bit.

"Hell no," I said with a slight laugh. "We talked a lot which was good. I even brought up all the stuff that I heard about him."

"Oh shit, you did?" She asked. "What did he say? Was he nervous?"

"Well, his phone kept going off, so it was pretty obvious that someone was trying to get in touch with him. When I asked him about it though, he played it cool and basically confirmed everything without saying too much. He made it clear he's not looking to be committed and I told him I wasn't either," I explained.

"That's good," she said. "So are you just gonna take it slow or do you like him?"

"I don't know yet," I said. "He tried to come upstairs but I shut that down quick. I plan on giving him another call though."

Stella's eyebrows raised and she smiled. "Good! It's about time you go and get yourself some," she said.

I looked around, glad to see that no one was where we were. Stella could be a little loud at times and we needed to make sure that we were professional. "Shh," I said. "I don't know about all that yet. I'm just figuring it out."

"Ok, whatever you say," she said with a smirk. "I gotta go take care of something so I'll let you get to your patient. Check in with me later."

"No problem," I said.

The rest of the afternoon kicked my ass. I thought he morning had been a little rough, but the afternoon had nothing on it. We had a bunch of patients who'd all gone on vacation together and came back with some kind of foreign bug that was tearing up their insides. I had to put them on all kinds of medicines to ease their symptoms while I waited for their test results to come back. By the end of the shift, I was glad for the two days off that I had coming up.

When I left the hospital, I stopped by my favorite wine store and picked up two bottles, one red and one white. I was going to be in the house and I knew that I'd get a craving for some at some point.

I spent my first day off doing the one thing that I never really had time to do; sleep. I woke up and made myself some breakfast and then took a nap. It was pretty much like that all day long. I didn't try and run any errands or anything. I just took the alone time to myself.

Being that I was always so used to being at work, relaxing wasn't something that I was good at. It was nice to spend the day sleeping but by my second day, I felt like I was going stir crazy. I cleaned up my whole apartment and then sat down to catch up on TV. I thought about what I could do.

Stella was working the late shift so she wouldn't be free. It finally crossed my mind that I should give Christian a call and see what he was up to.

When I called him initially, he didn't answer but he called me back after a few minutes. He said that he had meetings until later but he was free for dinner. I didn't feel like going back out so I suggested that we do takeout and a movie at my place. He said that he was down for it and told me that he could stop and get whatever I wanted if I texted it to him.

Later on that evening, Christian showed up to my apartment. He said that he wanted to surprise me with a movie and I asked him to stop and grab some Chinese food before he came.

He knocked at the door a little after nine o'clock.

"Hey, how are you?" I asked as I greeted him with a hug. I didn't know if he was coming straight from work or not but I planned on being comfortable even if he was wearing a suit. I'd thrown on a pair of jeans and a t-shirt. I'd also put on a little makeup so that I wasn't completely casual.

"I'm good, and you?" he asked as he stepped inside. "Wow," he commented as he looked around my condo, "this place is huge. And look at the view from the window. You can see everything."

"It was the reason that I took it," I said. "Hand me the bags. I can set the food up in the living room."

I showed him over to the couch and we sat down. I headed into the kitchen to grab some plates and things for us, plus one of the bottles of wine that I'd brought the day before.

"So," I began as I sat back down, "what movie did you bring?"

He laughed a little bit. "You know, I almost thought you were joking about bringing a movie. You know everyone just watches stuff online nowadays."

"I know," I said. "But I wanted to see what your taste in movies is like."

"I see," he chuckled. "Well, believe it or not I brought one of my favorites: Set It Off."

My eyes got wide. "With Queen Latifah?" I asked.

"Is there another one?" He responded. He pulled it out of his suit jacket. "I've seen it more times than I can count."

"Wow, I would've never picked you out to like movies like this," I said.

"Don't let the suit and tie fool you," Christian said with a smirk.

We started watching the movie and eating the food that he'd brought over. It was nice to hang out with Christian, especially when we had the same taste in movies. We were about twenty minutes or so away from the ending of the film and we'd been cuddled up the entire time. Something about being in the darkness together must have stirred something inside of us because when I sat up, Christian leaned in and kissed me, and I didn't stop him.

His soft lips had the faintest scent of cocoa

butter. His cologne wafted up my nose as the two of us sat on the couch kissing. He gently bit my lips which turned me on and our tongues touched a few times.

Things were going cool until it felt like Christian was trying to do too much. He started feeling on my body through my jeans, and that was alright, but I felt him trying to gently push me onto my back. He tried a few times and I used my hand to stop him, but he kept going, so I used a little bit of force to push him back and break the kiss.

"What's wrong?" he asked. He looked concerned.

"I...um...I think you should leave," I said quietly.

Now the look on his face was one of confusion. "Why? Did I do something wrong?"

"No, it's not you," I said honestly. It was difficult for me to put into words what I was feeling. I wanted to sleep with him but I still wanted to take some time to figure out what that really meant. I was risking a lot with Christian and I felt like I needed more time before I went that far. "I'm just...I don't want you to get the wrong impression or anything. I'm not ready for all of that yet."

"Alright," he said with a slight nod, "we can take it slow." He tried to lean back into kiss me more but I put my hand on his chest to stop him.

"I think you should go," I said a little more firmly.

"Ok, cool," he said. He stood up and grabbed his stuff. He didn't seem like he had an attitude or anything. I walked him to the door and he leaned down and planted a kiss on my cheek.

"Have a good night," he said.

"You too," I responded.

After I closed the door behind him, I headed into my bedroom and threw myself down on the bed. I couldn't believe myself. That fine ass man was in my house ready to do things to me and I'd kicked him out because of what...because I couldn't get out of my own head? It didn't make sense, even to me. I knew then that I had to find a way to get over my issues.

CHAPTER 4

Stella called me early the following morning and asked me if I wanted to get coffee with her before we went in since we were working the same shift. I was already up and was about to head out anyway so I told her we should meet at one of our favorite coffee places and grab some food before we went in. She agreed.

The coffee place was only a block away from the hospital so I just took a cab straight there. When I got there Stella was standing outside. I didn't know if anything was wrong or not, but she sure looked like it.

I walked up to get and greeted her. "Good morning," I said with a smile.

"Morning," she mumbled back. "You ready?"

I was confused and the look on my face showed it. "Yeah...sure," I said.

We headed inside the coffee shop and got our breakfasts. I had a muffin and a coffee and Stella had a bagel. The entire time that we were waiting to place our orders, Stella didn't say much. I tried to spark a conversation with her but she'd just respond with one word answers or just not say anything. Once we got out food, we decided to walk to the hospital to eat it.

"Are you alright?" I asked as we walked. "And don't give me none of that "I'm fine" mess cause we both know it's a lie."

Stella wasn't looking at me but she rolled her eyes. Finally she took a deep breath and began to speak. "I found out that I didn't get the promotion," Stella announced.

My eyes went wide with shock. "What? How? Who told you? Do you know who did get it?" I couldn't believe that she'd been skipped over for the job that she'd been working so hard for.

"I found out yesterday before I left," she said. She sounded defeated which was nowhere close to normal for her. "And to add insult to injury, they gave it to Ashley."

"Ashley?" I asked loudly. "How the hell are they gonna give it to Ashley and you've been here longer than she has? You don't have as many errors as she does, and her record isn't as clean as yours."

"I know," I said. "And when I brought all of that up to Dr. Hill, he basically said that the decision was made but he knows that I'll eventually get something."

"Damn, that's messed up," I said. Stella and I were at the corner where the hospital was and were about to head down the block when a car pulled up ahead of us. I wouldn't have paid it any attention but I saw the passenger side door open and watched as Ashley got out. Stella and I saw her lean back in and kiss whoever was driving the car.

We were walking at a normal pace but I sped up a little bit, just to see who she was kissing. Sure enough, Christian was the driver of the car. It wasn't the same one that he'd driven me in the other night but it was him.

Immediately I felt hurt. I felt like a fool. I'd kicked him out of my house the night before, only for him to end up as some other woman's house? I couldn't believe it. It was obvious that they'd slept together. Why else would he had been dropping her off at work?

"Did you see that shit?' I asked Stella.

I looked up at her and the look on her face was one of anger. "Yeah I did," she said. "And I bet that's the reason that she got *my* promotion." Stella was pissed off. She was breathing all hard. "Ashley's been this way since she came to the hospital. You should hear some of the shit that I've heard about her. She's a hoe. She's been with security guards, doctors, everyone."

I was only halfway listening to Stella. I knew that she had a right to be upset about everything that was happening, especially since she didn't get the promotion that she'd been going after but I was feeling bad for my own reasons that had nothing to do with that.

Christian and I weren't dating, but I still found myself hurt. I mean damn, he couldn't have waited a day or two before he moved on with the next one. He could have at least fucked with someone outside of the hospital. It was just my luck to walk up onto the show that they were putting on.

"Are you listening?" Stella asked, interrupting my thoughts.

"My bad girl, I got caught up in my head," I said. "What were you saying?"

"It's fine," Stella said, "I was just going off about Ashley. What's on your mind though? You look like you've seen a ghost."

I sighed. "Christian came over last night," I told her. The look on her face was of excitement but I quickly shut it down. "Not like that."

"So what happened?" she asked.

"Things got a little hot and heavy so I asked him to leave before I did something that I didn't want to do," I explained. "All we did was kiss. But after I kicked him out of my bed, it looks like he ended up in hers."

Ashley hadn't seen us since we were behind her. She walked into the hospital ahead of us. "I wouldn't take it too seriously," Stella said. "He probably had blue balls after being with you, and a man like that ain't gonna go to sleep that way.'

"That's true," I said. I didn't sound too convinced.

"This is just more of a reason why you know you can't take him seriously," she said. "That's what you need though. You can't take anything with him on a serious note until it seems like he's being more serious about it. That's how you protect yourself."

The more Stella spoke, the more I realized how right she was. "You know what, you do have a point," I said. "We did kind of establish from jump that we weren't looking for anything serious. He's free to do what he wants. I shouldn't have let it bother me."

"I agree," Stella said as we entered the hospital. Stella and I made our way upstairs. While walking down the hall we spotted Ashley. Stella decided to stop and speak to her. I hoped that she wasn't gonna call her out for what happened.

"Ashley, do you have a moment?" Stella asked. Ashley had been leaning against the wall texting or something and looked up when she saw us. She walked over to the other side of the hallway where we were.

"What's up?" Ashley asked. I didn't know how she could walk in her too-tight skirt.

"I just wanted to say congratulations," Stella said with a smile. "I heard about your promotion."

Ashley got a snide look on her face. "Thank you, Stella," Ashley said. I thought for sure we were in the clear until Ashley started speaking again. "I know how badly you wanted this. I'm sure they'll find something for you...eventually."

Stella rolled her eyes. "I was just trying to be professional," Stella began, "but if you want to go there, we can. You and I both know that you didn't deserve that promotion."

Ashley folded her arms over her chest. "Oh really? So then why am I the one with the pay increase and you're still out here looking for something to do?" She was a firecracker. That was for sure. It didn't seem like either of them were on the verge of backing down. I put my hand on Stella's arm to try and try and pull her away, but she ignored it and took a step towards Ashley.

"Ashley, we both know how you got that promotion," Stella said with a smirk, "probably the same way you get everything else: on your back."

Ashley's eyes got wide and then they narrowed as she looked back and forth between Stella and me. "You're just jealous that I got what you want," Ashley said. She turned her head towards me. "Even you," she said to me. "Christian needs a woman, not some little girl who plays games."

I didn't understand why the hell she'd added me into the mix but all of that stuff about me trying to hold Stella back went out the window.

Stella took another step towards Ashley. Ashley unfolder her arms and poked Stella hard in the chest. "Don't walk up on me," she said in an angry tone.

Stella was fuming mad now. She reached out her hand and grabbed Ashley roughly by the arm. Ashley had her hand up like she was about to swing so I reached out to grab her.

"What is going on here?!" A loud female voice stopped all of us. We quickly let one another go and turned to see who it was.

"I don't even wanna know! I can't believe this. What if there had been patients around?" Dr. Camila Houghton was one of the hospital higher ups. She happened to be walking passed us as everything was happening. In all honesty, as much as I hated to be caught in something so unprofessional, I was glad that someone stopped it before it got too far along.

Stella and Ashley both opened their mouths

to speak but Dr. Houghton was having none of it. "I don't want to hear it! Acting like children when we're supposed to be professionals. All three of you need to go upstairs to see administration and tell them what happened. I will be double checking later on, so I'll know if you don't go." She stood there looking more like a principal than a doctor and watched as we walked down the hall towards the elevator.

The ride upstairs was silent. Stella and Ashley kept throwing nasty looks at one another and I just rolled my eyes whenever I looked at Ashley. The tension was thick to say the least.

When we got to the office, we were seated by a secretary until we could head inside. I felt like I was back in high school or something like that. I knew that we'd behaved unprofessionally, but Ashley was on some other shit. Stella was just trying to be nice to her and she took that and ran with it, even throwing me into the mix.

After a few minutes of awkward silence, we were shown into the large office that belonged to one of the hospitals HR people.

"Well, this is something else," began Mr. Gold. He was an older gentleman in his early 50s with kind eyes and a warm smile. He seemed to be nice enough but I was annoyed with having to be there in the first place. "Please, have a seat. All three of you."

He had three chairs laid out in front of his large, oak desk. The office was decorated nicely with degrees on the wall and pictures of who I assumed to be his family members here and there.

Mr. Gold sat behind the desk and stared at us as if he was waiting for someone to speak. When no one did, he decided to get the conversation started.

"Dr. Houghton has already given me a call," he began. "She didn't get into the specifics but from what I understand, there was an altercation of some sort. This process doesn't have to be that long. I just need to know what happened."

Another full minute of silence went by. Mr. Gold leaned back in his chair as though he had the most patience in the world. Neither Stella or I said anything so after a while, Ashley started talking.

"Honestly, I don't know why I'm here," Ashley began. She leaned forward in her chair a little bit. "I didn't do anything wrong. This was just something that went too far for no reason."

"And what exactly did happen?" Mr. Gold asked. "There must have been a reason because Dr. Houghton said that she thought she might have needed to call security to get the three of you off of one another."

I didn't need to look at Stella or Ashley to know that they were probably showing the look of embarrassment on their faces that I had on mine.

"Mr. Gold, this is just a case of jealousy that went too far," Ashley said. "Dr. Frasier is jealous that I got the promotion that she's been working for. Dr. Jameson is still a resident and I believe that she may have gotten the wrong impression about a person that we were both interested in."

I rolled my eyes and was glad that no one had seen it. I couldn't believe that this chick was playing the jealousy card as though that's how the situation got started.

Mr. Gold turned his head towards me. He should have been a cop or something because he definitely knew how to play everything close to the chest. "So, Dr. Jameson, is this true? Who

is this person that seems to have sparked everything between you two?"

I figured that Ashley probably hadn't
thought about that part. If I was the jealous
type, I would have spilled the beans about her
and Christian right then and there. This little
scuffle in the hallway would have seemed like
nothing in comparison to a board member
sleeping with a doctor, especially one who'd just
been promoted.

"The person isn't important," I deflected. "I
was just stepping in to try and defend my friend
and colleague once I saw that things between
them were going the wrong way. Honestly, I
think it's just some stuff that got blown out of
proportion."

"I agree," Stella said. "I admit that we were
too loud and maybe it was just too early in the
morning for the conversation that we were
having. I do apologize. It's not something that I
plan on doing again."

I was glad that Stella chimed in to back my
story up. I knew that even if Ashley went first, it
would still be Stella and I versus her and two
heads were always better than one.

Mr. Gold asked us a couple more questions

to try and figure out what happened but he ultimately let us off with a warning and said that he'd just put a note into each of our personnel files saying that we'd spoken.

We left the office and Ashley sped ahead of us to get away. I was sure that she didn't want to spend any more time with us than we did with her. I was glad to rid of her.

Once we'd gotten far enough away from the office, Stella stopped me.

"Thanks for having my back in there," she said sincerely. "I really appreciate it. I can't believe I let her take me out of character like that."

"No problem," I said. "It wasn't just your butt on the line."

"Why didn't you tell him about Christian?" she asked. "You could have blown the lid off of it."

I shook my head. "Nah, that's not my style. We don't do that where I'm from," I said. "We had a strict no snitching policy. Honestly, it probably would have done more harm than help. You might never get a promotion if you have something big on your record."

"That's true," she said with a nod. Stella

looked down at her watch. "Hey, I gotta run. This has put me way off schedule and I know you have to be too. Let's get our days started and then we can check in with each other a little later."

"Alright, sounds good," I said.

CHAPTER 5

It had been a couple of weeks since the incident with Ashley and I was glad that things had calmed down. Thankfully it didn't seem like too many people knew what went on so the rumor mill was quiet. Stella and I kept things cordial with her whenever we saw her. Ashley was one of those overly dramatic people who could take a small moment and run with it. I didn't want to give her any more ammunition to use against me or Stella. I was just glad to be putting that whole situation behind me.

In deciding to move on from the situation, I also made the choice not to speak to Christian. He'd called and texted me more than a few times over the last few weeks but I hadn't reached back out to him. It wasn't that I was upset with him, or even Ashley for that matter. I just didn't want the drama. I hadn't even slept with him and there was already a situation involving another woman. I wasn't with it at all.

I had an early morning shift that day but I didn't mind it because it was over a little after two in the afternoon. I was glad to be leaving work as I stepped out into the heat of the midafternoon. The sun was beaming down and there wasn't too much of a breeze.

I didn't want to waste my entire day so I decided to go home and take a little nap to refresh myself. When I woke back up I decided to work out since I hadn't had a chance to do it that morning before I went in. The sun was still out and it was burning up outside. I decided that instead of running through the park like I normally did, I'd go to the gym close to my apartment.

My neighborhood was definitely one of the nicer ones. I loved the convenience of having the gym in walking distance of my house even though I wasn't technically a member. The hospital had some kind of hook up with the gym so a lot of the employees get discounts. I'd been using a guest pass to go there from time to time.

I got up out of bed and changed into my workout gear: black running tights, black and white sneakers, and a gray tank top. I tied my hair up in a ponytail and headed out the door.

As I walked down the street, I was glad that I'd made the choice to head to the gym. It was way too damn hot out to try and run. I'd already started to sweat a little just from the walk to the gym.

I headed inside of the two-story building, glad for the air conditioning once I was there. I walked over to the reception desk and handed the woman behind the counter the little card that was my guest pass. I waited for her to hand it back to me so I could grab a towel and head inside, but she started typing some stuff into the computer.

"Is everything alright?" I asked as I removed one of my headphones.

"Sorry about this," she said, "but it looks like this guest pass has expired."

I screwed up my face at her. "Are you sure? I thought it had another month on it," I said. I was sure that I'd double checked it before I left the house.

"I'm sorry, but the policy changed a while ago so now the passes only work for a certain number of visits. It looks like you've used all of yours," she explained. "If you'd like, we have a few representatives around if you were interested in joining the gym."

I could have joined the gym but I hadn't really planned on doing it that day. "It's alright. I didn't even bring my debit card with me," I said. I was about to turn and leave when a deep voice behind me spoke up.

"She can use my guest pass," someone said. I looked up and it was Christian, of all people. He was wearing a pair of black sweatpants and a sleeveless white shirt. He held his hand out to the woman and passed his membership card to her.

"I don't need you to do this," I said. "I was just gonna go get my debit card so I could join."

"It's alright," he said. "My guest pass is just a good as a regular membership. I'm a V.I.P. here."

The woman behind the counter handed him back his ID and then handed me a new guest pass. It was a different color than the one that I had before. She explained that the new pass had no limitations on how many times I could visit and I had unlimited access to the gym, but only this one location.

"Thank you," I said as we walked into the main area of the gym. "I didn't need you to do that for me though."

"Like I said, no problem," he said. He waved his hand to downplay it. "I was about to head to the V.I.P area if you wanted to join me."

The V.I.P. section of the gym was reserved for the members who paid more for their membership than everyone else. It came along with certain privileges like private washrooms and unlimited personal training. I'd never been over there though.

"I'm fine," I said. I hadn't planned on doing anything extra so I didn't need to go to his section. "I just came to run." I put my head-phones in my ear and walked over to the tread-mills. I found an empty one and stepped onto it. I selected a simple workout and set my speed.

Out the corner of my eye, I could see that Christian hadn't gone to the other area. He'd followed me over to the treadmills and was running on the one next to me. I didn't even turn my head to acknowledge him.

I'd been running for a few minutes and had gone from a light jog into a decently paced run. It wasn't until I increased my speed against that I realized what Christian was doing. Every time I went faster, so did he. He was trying to compete with me.

I finally turned my head to him. I had to admit that he looked cute with a little sweat on his face. I smirked at him and then reached down to my machine to increase the speed again. This time I went up more than the one or two clicks that I'd gone up before. He matched me and managed to keep up. I was a naturally competitive person so I wasn't about to let myself lose. I kept pushing the speed up, faster and faster. I could feel my feet slamming into the treadmill with every new step. I watched Christian's breath speed up until finally he couldn't take it anymore.

He pressed the slow down button on the machine until it came to a stop. He rode it and came off the end, bending over and supporting himself with his hands on his knees as he took deep breaths. I slowed my machine down too and climbed off of it to catch my breath as well.

I was still trying to catch my breath but I couldn't help but to start laughing at him. He might have been able to keep up with me but it definitely took more out of him than it did me.

"You're fast," Christian said as he finally recovered. "Real fast."

"I've been running since I was in school. I was on the track team," I said. "What are you about to go do now?"

"I'm just following your lead," he said with a smile. "So, what are *we* doing next?"

I smirked at him. "Alright," I said. "Let's head to the mats to stretch."

Christian and I joked as we walked over the rack and grabbed Yoga mats. I was walking ahead of him and I could practically feel his eyes on me in my running tights as we moved. I didn't mind it though. In fact, if he was in front of me, I'd probably try and check him out too. Christian was sexy. I had to admit that to myself.

We got down on the mats in front of mirrors. He started stretching on his own and I did the same. I didn't really work out with people often so it was silent between us for a while before he spoke.

So...um...I heard about what happened between you and Ashley," Christian said.

"Oh," I said as I kept stretching. If he was looking for more than that, he'd have to steer the conversation. It was definitely something that I was trying to put behind me.

"I just wanted to say thank you for not throwing me under the bus," he said. "I'm not in violation or anything for having slept with Ashley, but it's definitely not a good look either."

"It's fine, you don't have to thank me," I said as I moved into a new position. "Honestly, there was no need to bring you into it at all. I wasn't even sure why Ashley took it in that direction."

"Who knows?" he asked as he got down on the floor. "Ashley has always been that way; selfish and always ready to do the most." I wasn't looking in his direction but when I could see out the corner of my eye that he was looking at me, most likely waiting for a response. "I also wanted to let you know that Ashley and I aren't a thing for a while. That little incident with you two proved to me what I'd been thinking all along. I should have been more upfront with you about it."

"I promise you I'm not mad," I said as I stood up to move into a new position. "You're grown and can do what you want. We said that the first time we went out."

"Yeah, that's true," he said. He stood up and stopped stretching. "I'd like to take you out again...if you're still interested that is?" He smirked.

"I'll have to think about it," I said. I saw his face drop, but he recovered quickly.

"Alright," he said. "A slow yes is better than a quick no." He paused as he bent down to grab his mat. "I'm about to go head over to the weights so I'll leave you to it."

"OK," I said. Christian turned and walked away. I watched his reflection in the mirror. I felt myself getting a little turned on by the way that his clothes hugged his muscular body. He was handsome as hell and he knew it.

I finished my workout and headed back to my apartment. I couldn't believe it, but it felt like it had gotten hotter since I'd been in the gym.

As I walked, I toyed around with the possibility of going out with Christian again. I decided to throw caution to the wind and just go out. Part of me wanted to spite Ashley. I put the incident with her behind me but it still annoyed me that I'd let her take me so out of character.

I needed to avoid drama this time around. I decided that the best thing for me to do would be to play this very close to the chest. I didn't plan on telling anyone that I was going to go out with Christian, not even Stella. If we kept it between the two of us, we'd be able to avoid the mess.

I pulled out my phone and sent him a quick text message.

I thought about it and I'm down to go out again. Let me know when and where and I'll be there.

CHAPTER 6

I had just finished up in the clinic and was heading upstairs to start my rounds. I had spent the rest of the previous day relaxing after my workout so I was refreshed when I went into the hospital the next day. I stepped off the elevator and spotted Stella. She was speeding down the hallway and had her head in her iPad.

"Stella," I called out to her. She didn't seem to hear me so I walked quickly to catch up with her. I tapped her on the shoulder.

"Hey," she said as she turned around. "What'd you say?"

"I said hey," I said with a smile. "Are you alright? You seem a little off."

"Yeah, I'm fine," she said. "I'm just busy

with the details for the fundraiser. I knew it was gonna be a lot of work but damn."

"I'm sure you'll pull through," I said. "I'm about to go make my rounds but let me know if you need anything."

"No problem," she said.

I headed off and grabbed the charts to prep for my next round of patients. When I first started working there, I'd made the mistake of trying to remember everything about the patients. I ended up making a few small mistakes here and there and Stella had to correct me. She told me that while our hand-writing might have been crappy, doctors took great notes and I needed to learn to rely on the charts and not my brain.

I finished up my shift a couple of hours later. I was glad to be done because I had plans after work. I told Christian that we should do some-thing simple so he suggested dinner and a movie. I left the hospital and headed towards the theater that we'd agreed to meet at. It was far away from the hospital so the chances of us running into anyone that we knew were really slim.

Christian was dressed casually in jeans and a

pair of black and gray sneakers. I was wearing a pair of light blue jeans and flats.

"Hey," he greeted me with a hug and a kiss on the cheek.

"I was this close to being late," I said. "There was traffic for my cab."

"Oh well, you made it on time," he said. "How was your day?" We started to head into the theater to pick up the tickets that he'd purchased. We'd picked out a comedy movie to see.

"It was good," I said. "Stella was running around all day working on stuff for the hospital fundraiser."

"Yeah, she's been doing a good job with that," he said. "Are you going?"

"I wasn't planning on it, but I know I have to go since Stella is in charge" I said. "I know you'll be there since you're on the board."

"I was hoping you'd say that. I want you to be my plus one," he said. He stuck his card into the machine and waited for our tickets to print. "What do you say?"

"Well, that sounds good," I said. "It shouldn't be a problem since we're keeping things casual."

"I agree," he said with a smile.

After the movie, Christian and I headed to a diner style restaurant that served breakfast all day but also had drinks. The food was delicious and the conversation was great as well. We spoke about the movie and got to know one another better.

"Here we are," Christian said as we pulled up outside of my apartment building. After dinner he offered to drive me back to my place. It didn't make any sense for me to take another cab.

"Thanks for the ride," I said.

"Not a problem. Text me when you get in safely," he said. I didn't know what it was, but I felt intrigued by the fact that Christian hadn't tried to come upstairs with me the way that he had before. It felt like there was less pressure on me this time around.

I leaned over and pulled him close to me in a kiss. He didn't try and fight it. The kiss turned more intense than I thought it would but neither of us did anything to stop it. It wasn't until I felt his hand creeping up on my thigh that I decided we should stop.

I jerked my head back from him.

"Um...there's parking around the corner," I said.

I felt like a teenager. Christian and I laughed like kids as he drove the car around the corner. We headed into my building and as soon as the elevator doors closed, it was on. We couldn't keep our lips off of one another. We got up to my apartment and I unlocked the door and we headed inside.

Christian and I wasted no time, heading straight for the bedroom. I was turned on, but it had been so long since I'd done this that I was fine with him taking the lead on things. He closed the bedroom door behind us and then picked me up and dropped me on the bed with little effort.

I scooted back and kicked off my flats. He unbuttoned the shirt that he was wearing, exposing his muscular chest with a little hair in the middle. Slowly he climbed onto the bed next to me. He leaned in and started kissing me again, softer this time. His kisses moved from my lips down to my neck. I tilted my head to the side to give him more access.

As he licked and sucked at my neck, his big hands started rubbing on my thigh and working their way up to my jeans. I could tell that he knew what he was doing. The way that he removed my belt and unzipped my jeans with ease told me that experience was one thing he wasn't lacking.

I slipped out of my jeans and Christian stood up to remove more of his clothes. His jeans dropped to the floor with a small thud and he stood in front of me wearing only a pair of dark gray boxer briefs. I could make out the imprint of his dick which was getting harder and harder.

He climbed back onto the bed and hovered over me. There was a little light coming in through the window so we could see one another. I was only wearing my bra and panties by that point. He ran his index finger down my stomach a few times, slow and sensually. He stopped the finger at my panty line and slowly started to peel them off of me. I lifted my body so he could get them all the way off.

Christian moved me so that my back was on the pillows against my headboard. He started massaging my thighs and slowly took his fingers and started to massage my pussy. I hadn't gotten any in a while so my body was ready. He would stick his fingers into me and then pull them out slowly, each time getting deeper and deeper. I started to moan a little bit but he kept going. It wasn't until my legs jerked open a little more that he finally stuck his head between them and started to eat me out.

Christian may have come across as prim and proper on a daily basis, but in the bedroom he was something else. The man was putting in work. I put my hands on the sides of his face to try and stop him because it felt almost too good. He kept right on going, licking and sucking at me like I was his favorite meal.

My hands clenched into fists with my first orgasm. I felt everything tighten up and then immediately become loose again. I was breathing hard like I was back at the gym.

I didn't even have much time to recover because before I knew it, Christian was sliding a condom on and heading towards me. I'd been laying there with my eyes closed after the orgasm so I didn't even realize that he'd taken his underwear off.

I looked down at his dick and saw that it was a nice size. It was a little longer than average but definitely on the thicker side. The look on his eyes was one of lust and though I was definitely ready for it, I wasn't about to let him just stick that thing into me.

Christian and I started kissing again and I managed to flip him over onto his back. I was ready to get it in with him but I wanted to be in control. I decided that riding him would be the best since I needed to get used to him.

We kissed and he played with my nipples, squeezing each of them between his fingers. It turned me on even more. I maneuvered my body that I could slowly take him inside of me, inch by inch. He held onto my waist and slowly pulled me down on top of him. I paused, getting used to the feeling before I started to slowly rock my hips back and forth. After a minute or two it started to feel better and I built up a rhythm. I moaned out loud as his hands gripped my body and ran all over me.

"Ooh," I cooed. I placed my hand on his chest to steady myself as I moved. I lifted my body higher off of him and came down with more force and pressure. He didn't mind it though. He put his hand on the side of my hip and pulled me back down on to him. I could feel his midsection raising off the bed with each stroke as he worked himself in and out of me.

"Fuck," Christian moaned after a few minutes. My eyes were closed but I could still feel his focus on me.

His aggression picked up and I could tell that he was close to coming. He was working his hips in and out of me quickly. I was feeling amazing. Christian's thickness filled me all the way up and for a few minutes I couldn't' remember why I'd waited so long to have sex again. He wrapped his arm around my back and pulled me closer to him as he sat up. Our eyes connected as he stroked in and out of me.

"Oh...oh...." I moaned loudly. I could feel my body close to another orgasm and before it even hit me, I already knew that it was gonna be more intense than the first one. Christian matched my speed and before I knew it, both of us were coming at the same time. We cleaned up and headed to sleep.

When I woke up the following morning, Christian was still asleep in my bed. I was surprised because I pegged him to the "leave before she wakes up" kind of guy. I peeled his arm from over my body and got my day started.

I didn't know what he had planned but I needed to get ready for work.

I knew that I would get him up before I left the house so I decided to just leave him alone. I climbed into the shower and got dressed when I got out. Heading into the kitchen I put on a pot of coffee and threw a bagel into the toaster.

After a few minutes Christian came out of the bedroom. He had a sleepy look on his face but looked well. He was halfway dressed and slipping his shirt on his body. He came into the kitchen and sat down at the table across from me.

"There's coffee in the pot," I said. "Good morning."

"Morning," he said. He headed over to the coffee pot where I'd already pulled out an extra mug for him. "How'd you sleep?"

I sipped my coffee and looked at him. "Well, and you?"

"Like a baby," he said with a smirk. "I was thinking that I could give you a ride to the hospital if you'd like."

I shook my head. "Nah, it's alright. I usually just take a cab," I explained.

"Oh, alright," he said. "How about we grab some breakfast before you go in?"

Almost right on cue, my bagel popped out of the toaster. "I usually just have a bagel and some fruit. I can put one on for you if you want," I said.

"No...no," it's alright. He took a sip of the coffee and stared at me with confusion.

"What is it?" I asked.

He just shook his head. "Nothing, you're just something else," he said.

"What does that mean?" I asked.

"Well, usually women love for me to stick around. I usually wake up and they've made breakfast or something like that to try and get me to stay," he said. "You're clearly not that type."

"Clearly," I agreed. "It's not disrespect or anything like that. I just want for us to be clear about what this is. Last night was...fun. And, as long as no one knows about this, it could be more of a regular thing."

"That sounds like fun," he said.

Christian and I both finished getting dressed. I was heading to the hospital and he said that he was going to go home and change his clothes before he went to work. We kissed passionately before he left and made tentative plans to try and do it again soon.

I went to work with a clear mind. I was feeling more stress free than I had in a long time. I didn't know if it was Christian or the sex but one of them had me going through work on cloud nine. I definitely felt more at ease about everything, especially since we'd agreed to keep everything on the low. It was important for me to keep this situation as drama free as possible and he seemed to be with it. I think the fact that I knew that I wouldn't have the added headache of people in my business was making me feel at ease.

I couldn't deny it. Christian had put it down on me the night before. I knew that it was more than just the fact that I hadn't done it in a while. He really did know what he was doing and it turned me on. I hadn't even had a chance to pull out all of my nasty little tricks and what not. I was already looking forward to seeing him again.

If Stella noticed anything different about me that day, she didn't say anything about it. I managed to dodge her a couple of times to avoid questions and stuff.

I went home and took a shower to wash the day off of me. When I got out, I noticed that I had a text from Christian. He was being sweet and said that he missed me. I had a quick flash-back to the night before and realized that I was getting a little wet. I sent him a text back saying that I missed him too and couldn't wait to see him again.

Open up the door.

I quickly read the text from Christian and then read it again. I heard a knock at the door and headed to answer it, already sure of who it was on the other side. Standing there wearing an all gray sweat suit was Christian. He was holding a box of condoms in his hand and had a silly grin on his face.

"I was in the neighborhood," he said sarcas-tically He held the box of condoms up. "I'm trying to go through all of these tonight. You down?"

I grabbed him by the shirt and pulled him into my apartment.

CHAPTER 7

I usually hated working overnight shifts because they messed up my sleep schedule. However, I was more than glad to be working this one since Christian had messed up my sleep the night before and made me have to sleep all day. I didn't mind it though. Not to mention the fact that I would be working with Stella.

Overnights were usually quieter but because of the skeleton crew that was available, it could sometimes get rough. There were only a handful of doctors available to treat whatever was going on. I tried to avoid the emergency room when I did overnights.

I was just about to go to the staff only area

and heat up my lunch for the night. It was nothing fancy, just a sandwich. However, just as I was about to head out, one of the nurses coming back from her shift handed me a bag of what smelled like something delicious.

"What's this, Donna?" I asked her in confusion. "I didn't order anything."

"Benny, the security guard, asked me to bring it upstairs to you. He said that a delivery guy dropped it off downstairs for you," she explained.

"Do you know where it came from?" I asked.

"No," she said with a shrug before she walked off.

I sat the bag down on the counter and opened it up. There was a receipt on top that told me that Christian had bought the food and had it delivered. I pulled out my phone and sent him a quick text thanking him for buying it for me.

"Damn, what's that?" Stella walked up behind me and started inspecting the food. "You got Spanish food? Without me? You should have told me and I would have ordered with you."

"My bad girl. I was in such a rush," I lied.

Stella shrugged. "No problem...as long as I can have some," she said playfully. She looked down at her pager. "Before this thing goes off again I need to get something in my stomach."

"Come on then," I said.

There was more than enough food for one person. I was glad that it had come with plates and stuff. Stella and I took a little bit of every-thing that was there: rice, beans, plantains, and baked chicken. We sat at the back of the nurses' station to eat and talk.

"How's your shift been so far?" Stella asked. "I haven't even made it down to the E.R. yet. There was a situation in ICU."

"Oh really? What happened? Was is Mr. Wells again?" I asked. "And it's been mostly quiet down here."

"Yeah, it was him," she said as she ate her food. "That old man keep trying to pull out every damn tube in his body. Every shift says that they basically had to threaten to restrain him unless he stops."

I shook my head. "Some people are just stubborn like that," I commented.

"Speaking of stubborn," she asked with a devilish look in her eyes, "have you heard anymore from Christian? Or has he finally stopped hitting you up?

I almost choked on the rice that I was eating because it seemed like she knew something, but I was sure that she didn't. I quickly recovered to stop myself from seeming suspicious.

"It's been pretty quiet on that front," I lied. I hated that I couldn't tell Stella the truth. I knew that she only had my best interests in mind but it didn't make it any easier. I just knew that the best thing for me to do was to play things with Christian close to my chest. It hadn't been that long since he and I started whatever it was that we were doing and I didn't want to make it complicated.

"Well, I'm sure he'll come around," she said. "If you want him to that is."

"I'm just playing it cool," I said. "What's been going on with you? Any new flings?" I was eager to change the subject.

She rolled her eyes. "I thought for a little bit that I might have found someone I could get serious with but it turned out to be a fluke," she said. "We went out a couple of times and everything seemed to be fine but then he found out what I did for a living and ended things. I didn't even get a chance to sleep with him."

She looked genuinely disappointed. "I mean...is that a bad thing?"

"I guess not." She shook her head. "I just hate how guys are so intimidated by a woman who has her shit together."

"It's the same for all of the women here," I said. "I'm sure you'll find someone though."

"Oh, trust me, I will," she said. "And in the meantime I'm gonna have fun taking these dudes out for test runs," she added with a laugh.

I couldn't help but to laugh with her. "You're a whole mess, girl," I said.

"Oh well," she smirked.

Stella left me alone after a few minutes. Her pager went off and she had to make a run for it. It was nice to have a few minutes with her alone where we didn't talk about hospital stuff.

The rest of my shift went by quickly and uneventfully. I was glad for it too. By the time that six in the morning came around, I was more than ready to head out. I made my notes for the shift change and then headed downstairs to my car. I rarely got a chance to drive it since I liked taking cabs so much but when it came to overnights, I always drove.

The parking garage in the basement was halfway empty. There seemed to be a lot of cars coming and going, probably because everyone was switching shifts. I made my way down to the second level and headed towards my car. I got the shock of my life when I turned the corner and saw Christian leaning up against it.

I looked around and was glad to see that the closest people were still several yards away but they were walking in my direction. Christian had this goofy ass grin on his face.

"What the hell are you doing here?" I asked him as I rushed over to him. "Leaning up against my car and shit! What if someone sees you?" I reached into my purse and pulled out my keys. I quickly unlocked the door and told him to get inside.

"Christian, what the hell are you doing here? Someone could have seen you," I said. "You know I'm trying to keep this on the low."

"Damn, I can't just come and see you at work," he said in a playful way. "My feelings are hurt."

I tried to keep being mad at him but it

wasn't easy. From where my car was parked, someone would have to pretty much walk right up to the car to see who was inside of it.

"Why are you here so early?" I asked.

"I have a meeting at the hospital a little later," he said.

"And you just had to hang out on my car?" I asked.

"Damn, I ain't know it was really gonna be a problem for you," he said. "I just wanted to see you."

He was really playing up the whole fake offensiveness thing. "Oh please," I said as I rolled my eyes.

"I'm so hurt," he kept going. "You gotta make it up to me."

He said the last part flirtatiously and it turned me on. "Make it up to you how?"

"Well," he said as he looked down at his watch, "I do have some time to kill. We could go back to your place...unless you were trying to get it started here." He smirked but the look on his face was a serious one. I just stared at him but didn't say anything.

Christian's hands were in his lap. He undid his belt and buckle and slowly unzipped his pants. He was wearing a pair of black underwear. His hand slowly slipped into them as he started to massage himself to erection.

"I'm not fucking you in the hospital's parking lot," I said. He looked genuinely disappointed, but he didn't know what I did have planned for him. Without saying another word, I moved his hands and leaned down into his lap, taking all of him into my mouth.

It didn't take long for him to get hard then. I didn't know what had come over me but I was feeling adventurous. Something about the idea of getting caught was turning me on in such a way that I couldn't help but to give him head.

I tried not to make too much noise as my head bobbed up and down in his lap. I was glad that Christian had good hygiene. I hated when I was with a guy and they had weird smells or even worse, musk.

I knew my head game was the bomb, and Christian was finding out how true that was as I slurped him up and down and used my hands to jerk him off at the same time.

"Oh shit," he moaned. "Damn, Kallie. Suck that shit." Christian's moans made me glad that no one was around because he was getting louder and louder. I could feel his body starting to tense up as if he was close to coming and that was when I stopped.

"What?" He opened his eyes and looked at me. I knew he had just been on cloud nine. "Why'd you stop?" He started looking out the windows. "Is someone coming?"

"No," I said as I shook my head. "But you said you had time to kill, so why don't we head back to my place before your meetings?"

"I'll follow you in my car," he said. "Damn, you really know how to turn me on." He looked down at his dick which was still brick hard and now shiny because of my spit.

"You might want to give *that* a minute to go down some," I said as I pointed to his dick.

Christian and I headed back to my apartment and fucked the hell out of one another. He ended up being late for his meeting because he went to take a shower and then invited me in which led to another round. It felt good to be getting some on the regular again and it definitely didn't hurt that he knew exactly what he was doing.

Christian was making me feel like a teenager all over again. Over the next few days, he and I would sneak off and have sex whenever we could. I tried to tell him that we could have just done it in one of our cars, but he said that no one really went to their cars in the middle of the day, so it would look suspicious. He and I found our way into empty offices and closets. We couldn't get enough of one another.

Over time it was becoming more and more clear to me that Christian was taking this a little more seriously than I was. He would give me little intimate gifts here and there and he kept mentioning how much he enjoyed spending time with me. It was flattering to say the least, but I wanted him to keep our original agreement in mind. It was just supposed to be fun.

CHAPTER 8

The night of the hospital's fundraiser had finally arrived. Stella had been working her ass off for it and was really excited. She had been talking my ears off about the details of it for what felt like forever and some of her excitement had finally rubbed off on me. She'd been saying for a while that it was gonna be fancy. The dress code was formal which meant that I got the chance to buy a new dress.

Christian was just as excited about it. He'd double checked with me that we were still going with one another. I confirmed that we were but kept trying to push the fact that it was just a plus one kind of situation and not a real date. I was trying my hardest to keep things casual and calm but it felt like he kept pushing for more.

Christian and I were arriving at the party together. He'd been pushing for it to happen so I just went with it. He was outside of my apartment building in a black car that he'd gotten for us for the night. He said that it was too fancy of an event for us to just drive there.

I stepped off the elevator and headed into the lobby of my building. My doorman, Tommy, was sitting at his desk and put his newspaper down when her saw me.

"Oh my goodness! Dr. Johnson you look amazing," he said. He eyed me up in down in the same way that a grandparent looked at their grandkids.

I stopped walking and did a little spin for him. I was wearing a gray gown that was cinched at the waist and low cut in the front. I'd pulled my hair up into an elegant bun and had put on makeup and accessories. I had to practice walking around in my heels earlier in the day but it had all come together nicely. I loved that the silk dress hugged my curves and held onto my body in a classy but sexy way.

"Thank you, Tommy," I said. "I'll see you later."

"Have fun, and don't hurt anyone," he added with a wink.

I smiled at him before I stepped out of the building where there was a driver waiting to open up my door. I got into the back of the car and found Christian dressed in a tuxedo. He looked handsome as hell. He always gave off this feeling of wealth and arrogance but dressed in his designer suit, it was more than apparent that he was someone important.

We chopped it up in the back of the car on the way there. I told him that I was excited and he was glad that we were going together.

When we arrived we saw that they'd gone all out. They'd rented a large conference area at one of the hotels on Lake Michigan. It was right on the water and had a balcony that overlooked it. They'd gotten fancy balloons and decorations and had even laid out a red carpet. There was a huge entryway that allowed people to stop and take pictures the way that celebrities did for movie premiers and things like that.

I was planning on avoiding all of the hoopla and just heading straight in, but Christian insisted that we walk the carpet. We went back and forth about it for a few seconds but I ultimately gave in. We started to walk the carpet and Christian grabbed my hand in his. I wanted to snatch it away, but it would have looked awkward, especially since other people were around. Walking into the fundraiser was one thing but walking into it hand in hand was giving off some other vibe that I didn't really want to be giving off.

Christian and I stopped and posed for the cameras. We were all smiles but in between photos, I caught glances from several other people, mostly women. If looks could kill, I would have been a dead woman several times over.

We made our way into the main entrance hall and I was glad for it too because it finally gave me a chance to get away from Christian for a moment. I told him I'd be right back and tried to walk off but didn't make it too far.

"Kallie!" Stella was making her way from the other side of the room. She called my name loudly and I stopped in my tracks.

"Hey," I said awkwardly. "I love your dress." I wasn't lying either. She had on this beautiful champagne colored gown that really showed off her beautiful skin.

Stella wasn't impressed. She folded her arms up at me. "Mmm hmm," she said. "Thank you. So... you and Christian? How'd you go from not wanting to be here to showing up with him on your arms and why wasn't I told?"

I held up my hands to calm her, wishing that I'd been able to make it to the bar before she came to me. "It's not what it looks like," I pleaded.

"So what is it then? I thought we were friends," she said.

"And we are," I said. "He just needed a date, and so did I. It's casual, at least on my end."

Stella's eyes narrowed at me. "You're lucky I have to help host this thing or else I'd ask you more questions," she said. "I'll see you around tonight and be careful."

"Why?" I asked in confusion.

"Girl, you showing up with Christian was pretty much blood in the water," Stella said. "The women are already buzzing and I *know* some of them are jealous 'cause he's claiming you."

"He's not," I said firmly. "Actually, he's been

acting like this is something it's not. He was the one who wanted to hold hands and all that. I wanted to avoid the carpet. It's actually kind of annoying.

"The two of you showed up hand in hand and walked the carpet. That's a claim if I ever saw one in my life," Stella said. "But if he's getting the wrong impression, you should just tell him about it. He's not a one-woman kind of man from what it seems so he should get the message." I opened my mouth to say something but before I could, someone was calling for her. She apologized and said that she had to run.

I made my way over to the bar and ordered a cocktail. Christian soon found me and made his way over to the bar by me.

"There you are," he said as he reached me. He put his hand on my hip in what I thought was supposed to be an assuring way "I was looking for you."

"Yeah, I just wanted to grab a drink and I ran into Stella. She really outdid herself with this," I said. The bartender came over and handed me my drink. It was an open bar but there were a few cash tip jars. I threw some money in there. I took a sip of my drink as Christian ordered one for himself.

"Are you enjoying yourself?" he asked as he got his drink.

"Yeah, it's only been a few minutes," I said. "The music is nice though."

"I agree," he said as he took another sip. "You wanna come with me and meet some of the potential donors? You guys might all be off tonight but as a member of the board, I have to suck up to some people to get them to open their checkbooks."

Small talk with people that I didn't know wasn't my ideal night but we did come together so I decided to go along with it. Christian and I made our way to one of the other food tables in the room. When we got there an older gentleman was standing with a glass of champagne in his hand talking to some other people. I watched Christian slowly work his way into the conversation.

"Lionel, I'd like you to meet someone," Christian said. The older guy had a nice smile and bright gray eyes. "This is Dr. Kallie Jameson."

"Nice to meet you, Dr. Jameson," Lionel said. He took my hand in his and shook it.

"Same to you," I said.

"Lionel here is in the medical equipment business," Christian said. "He and I have worked together before outside of the hospital."

"And how do you two know one another?" Lionel asked with a smile.

Before I could open my mouth and say anything, Christian grabbed my hand and started to speak. "Kallie and I are dating," he said.

I was trying to keep my face normal but it was hard. "We're each other's dates," I said. I was trying my hardest to correct him without making it into a big thing. If Lionel noticed the tension that was coming off of me, he didn't let it slip.

Meeting Lionel was just the beginning of the night for Christian and I. It felt like he was parading me around in front of everyone and at one point I had to start making my own intro-ductions. Christian kept on telling people the wrong thing and I wasn't here for it. It got so bad that I ended up excusing myself from one of the conversations and headed into one of the hallways to get some air.

"Kallie, is everything alright?" I hadn't even heard the door open up again so I didn't know that Christian was creeping up behind me.

"What are you doing here?" I asked. "I said I'd be right back.

"Yeah, but you looked upset so I wanted to check on you," he said. He took a step closer and put his hand on my shoulder.

"Christian, we need to talk," I said. He took his hand off my shoulder and stared me in the eyes.

"What's up?" he asked. "Are you alright?"

I found myself getting upset because it was clear that he wasn't even aware in the slightest of what could be on my mind. "I'm fine, Christian," I snapped. "I just need you to stop doing what you were doing in there?"

"What are you talking about?" He looked confused. "I've been on my best behavior. If you're talking about that little thing with Diane, that's on her. She's a cougar so she'll flirt with any guy under 40."

I rolled my eyes. "No, not Diane. Us!" I

wasn't trying to be loud but I wanted him to know that I was being serious.

"What about us?" He got a doofy smirk on his face.

"Christian, you can't keep telling people that we're together, because we're not," I said. "I know this isn't the time or the place for this but I think we need to have a serious conversation about what's happening between us. I don't want you to think I'm not appreciative of you and what we do, but this is starting to feel way too serious, and I thought we both agreed to just keep it casual."

"But what's wrong with that?" he asked. "I like spending time with you, Kallie. I *been* cut off everyone else that I was dealing with, just to focus on you."

"But I didn't ask you to," I said. I was trying my hardest to get him to see things my way but it was like there was an invisible wall between us or something. "It's not fair for you to try and force this relationship on me. You're out there telling people that we're dating and you know how much I wanted to keep this on the low."

Christian didn't say anything and I almost lost my fucking mind. It was clear to me that while his eyes might have been focused on me, all he was doing was staring at me and not paying attention. I couldn't believe he had the nerve.

I rolled my eyes and started to walk away. Christian reached out and grabbed my hand.

"Kallie, my bad," he said. He pulled me closer to him and I tried to walk away. He took a step closer to me and started to kiss me all over my lips and neck.

"Christian, stop!" I said. I was trying to fight it but after a while it started to feel good. I shook my shoulders to try and get him off of me. "What if someone sees us?"

"Ain't that always the case with us?" he asked. He sneakily looked around and when he didn't see anyone, he led me over to a door that led to a staircase. He shut the door behind us.

"I can't believe we're doing this," I said. I might have been thinking it out loud but I was lowering my dress as Christian stuck his hand through the slit and up my panties.

15 minutes later I was stepping out of the stairway and heading towards the bathroom to fix my hair and makeup. I told Christian that he should just head right back into the party so

people wouldn't get suspicious about where had had been.

He and I had just finished a quick sex session. Christian might have been a problem in other areas of our situation but when it came to sex, there was never an issue.

As I made my way to the bathroom, I still couldn't get over my feelings about Christian. He was a great guy but I just didn't feel the connection with him the way that he felt it with me. He was nice and could be kind when he wanted to be but he was aggressive and arrogant. He made the decisions for the most part and just expected for me or whoever else to just go with them. He also treated himself like he was some kind of prize to be won. At times he gave off this "you should be glad to be with me" kind of attitude.

Even if all the problems with Christian could be fixed, it still wasn't that simple. Truth be told, I was resistant to him because I didn't want to put my heart out there to get broken again.

CHAPTER 9

The hospital's fundraiser ended up being a huge success. I was especially proud of Stella for being the organizer and for working too hard to turn it into what it was. When we went back into the party, I convinced Christian that it would be best for him to try and get donations instead of following behind me all night. He finally seemed to get it and left me alone for a while, which was refreshing.

I was off the day following the party and I was glad for it too. I managed to have a good time at the party once Christian left me alone. I left late and had a nice buzz by the time I got home so I was glad to be able to sleep for most of the following day.

Christian had been hitting me up but I hadn't really been too responsive to him. I didn't want things to be awkward but I also didn't really know what to say to him. He just didn't seem to understand where I was coming from. As it got closer to the night time, I finally decided to respond to his texts and accepted his invitation for him to come to my place.

Christian showed up at my apartment a little after seven o'clock. He leaned in for a kiss when he got there and I offered him my cheek. He tried to get me to go into the bedroom with him but I suggested that we watch a movie instead. He seemed disappointed but he gave in.

We were sitting on my couch, enjoying takeout and watching some movie but I could feel his eyes on me the whole time. He paused the movie and turned to me.

"What's wrong with you?" Christian asked. He was looking at me with confusion on his face. I turned to him and stared him in the eyes.

"What do you mean?" I asked, even though I had a pretty good idea of what he was talking about.

"You know what I mean, Kallie," he said with more force in his voice than before. "You're acting funny and I wanna know why."

I took a deep breath and sighed. "Christian, I still feel the same way that I felt at the fundraiser. Things are getting too serious and I thought we'd agreed to keep it casual."

Christian screwed his face up at me. "Why are you still on this?" he asked. "It is casual."

"No it's not," I said with a shake of my head. "Or at least it doesn't feel like it. It almost feels like we made a mistake by going to the fundraiser together. Now everyone has the wrong idea about us."

"And what's the right idea, Kallie?" Christian asked and I could practically feel the arrogance rising off of him. "You should be happy that I'm trying to take things further with you. I don't normally do this with anyone but you're special."

I rolled my eyes. I couldn't believe the nerve of him. Once again he was making it seem like I should have been happy that I wasn't one of the women that he just fucked and left alone.

"You need to relax," I said. "You're not listening to what I'm saying. I told you from the beginning that I was trying to take things slowly and not rush into anything. I also made it clear that I wanted this to just be a casual thing. Now you're trying to put pressure on me and what not. What's next? Taking trips together?'

Now it was his turn to roll his eyes. "And what would be so wrong with that?" he asked. He paused and shook his head. "Women always saying they want one thing and actually want another."

I was actually offended by that point. "We can't keep doing this if you're not gonna listen to me," I said in a firm tone. "And I mean that."

"So what does that mean, Kallie?" he asked. I could tell that he was getting more and more upset the longer that the conversation went on. I wasn't too calm myself.

"Christian, we might need to take a break from all of this," I said. "Maybe take some time and space and then try and come back in a few."

He shook his head. Christian leaned in close to me and before I could stopped him, he kissed me on the lips. I pushed him back.

"Christian! We're having a conversation," I said. "I'm trying to talk to you."

"I hear what you're saying," he said as he moved his hand slowly up my thigh and leaned in closer to me. "I really do. But I don't want us to take it that far. I can relax," he said.

He was face to face with me now and slowly leaned in to kiss me. I backed my head up some but he was persistent, and before I knew it, we'd fallen into a passionate kiss.

Just like the night before, I'd allowed Christian to stop what should have been a serious conversation with some kisses that turned into more. I knew that I needed to be stronger, but he just felt so good at times. I admitted to myself that we were never going to make any progress if I couldn't hold my ground and stop him from seducing me whenever I tried to talk to him.

Christian ended up staying the night. Like always, he offered to drive me to work the following morning, but I told him that it wasn't necessary. Things were a little awkward with us but I just pushed through it, not trying to let that energy mess up my work day.

When I got to the hospital I realized that it was my first shift since the fundraiser. There was something...different about everything when I got there. There wasn't tension in the air, but something else. I felt it from the minute that I walked into the building. A couple of people smirked at me like they were in on some joke that I didn't know about. Not to mention that if I got a dollar for every nasty look thrown my way, I would have been able to pay my rent for a few months.

"I feel like I walked into the Lion's Den," I said to Stella when I finally saw her. She looked like she'd taken some time since the fundraiser to relax. It was nice to see her not be as stressed out as she was before.

"What you mean? Stella asked. She was looking at a patient's chart as I approached her.

"It feels like everyone is treating me differently," I said. "I ran into some of the higher-ups on the elevator and they actually knew my name...and called me by it instead of glancing down at my nametag. Not to mention that if I didn't know who they were before, I'm *definitely* aware of who Christian slept with cause they keep throwing nasty glances my way."

"That's a damn shame," Stella said. "Grown ass women can't keep their emotions in check. Oh well, it shouldn't be too bad. It'll blow over in a few days. It's not like you guys were the biggest story coming out of the party."

"Oh really? What happened?" I asked.

"Girl, the hospital's vice president was drunk as a skunk. She managed to make it outside the party before she started throwing up everywhere. Her husband had to practically drag her away," Stella explained.

I couldn't help but to bust out laughing. Hospital parties were always interesting because we got a chance to see the people who normally acted all prim and proper finally let loose and the results usually were hilarious. "Are you serious?" I asked.

"Hell yeah," I said. "She took off the day after but it's not like anyone is gonna say anything to her. She is our boss after all."

"That's true," I said. I reached over the nurses' station and grabbed a patient's chart to start my day.

"I'm about to go upstairs for a meeting but let me know if you need anything," Stella said. "And Kallie, don't worry about any of this stuff. I know how it can be when your name is on everyone's lips but stuff like this doesn't last forever. It'll be a hot topic for a little bit but people are gonna move on after a day or two."

"Thanks, Stella," I said.

I went ahead and got my day started. I was glad that I didn't have to do any clinic stuff that day and only had to make my rounds with a few patients. Things were going fine for the most part. I even got a chance to assist on a surgery for the day but things took a turn for the worst when I spotted Ashley.

I had seen her a bunch of times the night of the party and she made sure to throw me a nasty glance every time that she saw me. I'd managed to avoid her that night, making sure that wherever I was, she was on the other side of the room. I definitely wasn't afraid of her, but I also knew that Ashley came with a certain level of drama attached to her that I didn't want.

"Dr. Johnson," Ashley had spotted me from down the hall and called out to me, "do you have a moment?"

I was mad that she'd seen me and I was so close to making it into another patient's room before she stopped me. I wasn't afraid of Ashley but I also didn't want to be confronted in the hospital by her, especially not with the way that everything happened between me her and Stella last time.

"Sure, Ashley," I said as she speed walked her way over to me.

There was an empty patient room close to where we were. She pushed her way into the door and I followed her, closing it behind us.

"Look, I'm not doing this," I said firmly. I crossed my arms over my chest and rolled my eyes. "If this isn't about a patient, I'm out." I made a move to step towards the door but she stepped in front of me and folded her arms as well.

I stepped back. I wasn't scared but I didn't want to be too closer to her in case she tried something. Ashley had proven once before that the hospital setting didn't really make much of a difference to her professionally.

"How long have you and Christian been dating?" Ashley asked. She looked me up and down like she was sizing me up. "It must have been for a while since you guys showed up to the fundraiser together."

"Jealous?" I asked. I couldn't help but to rub it in her face a little bit. "Not that it's any of your business, but Christian and I aren't dating. We're just friends."

"Oh please," Ashley huffed. "Everybody plays that "just friends" mess. I don't believe it. I know what kind of man Christian is and he ain't the friendly type. So, how long?"

I took a deep breath to try and calm myself down. I couldn't believe the nerve that Ashley had. If this was a couple of years ago before I was in the medical world, I would have beat her ass. However, I was an adult and needed to act like it.

"Ashley, I'm not telling you anything else. I said Christian and I are friends and that's it. If you wanna know anything else, ask him," I said. I walked up to her to head towards the door. Ashley might have been a lot of things but unless she was stupid, she'd get out of my way.

The two of us stared at one another, each waiting for the other to make a move. Finally, she sighed and stepped to the side allowing me out.

To say that I was frustrated by Ashley would be an understatement. I could barely finish up with my patients because I was so flustered. It didn't make any sense to me how sleeping with one man could cause so much drama. My entire day felt like it belonged to someone else and not me.

I found Stella a short while after my confrontation with Ashley and asked her if I could leave early for the day. She could tell that there was something wrong with me and tried to get me to talk to her but I made it clear that I just wanted to leave. When it was clear that I wasn't about to talk about it, she finally let me go.

On my way home, I stopped by the store and bought a bottle of wine. When I got to my house, I put my phone down on the counter in the kitchen and left it there for the rest of the day. I didn't want to be bothered by anyone for any reason at all. Stella and Christian had both hit me up multiple times, but I ignored them and everyone else.

‘

CHAPTER 10

It was the following morning and though I was speaking to people, Christian wasn't one of them. As I got up and headed out for my daily run, I decided to use it as an opportunity to clear my mind. It didn't make any sense the way that Christian was so in my head because of everything that was happening with us.

I left my building and headed towards the park that I usually ran through, though this time I decided to take a more scenic route to make my run longer. As I jogged I tried to think of what I could say to Christian to make him understand what I was saying and where I was coming from. He was more than reasonable so I couldn't understand why he wasn't getting what I was trying to say to him. The more that I thought about it, the more I realized that his arrogance was what was getting in the way. He really couldn't understand why I wasn't falling head over heels for him.

I was building up quite a sweat as I ran but the longer my run, the more it felt like I understood what I needed to do. I was planning out what to say to Christian and I made a commitment that no matter what happened, I wouldn't let him seduce me or anything the way that he'd done before. We needed to have a very serious conversation and I didn't want us to be interrupted, or at least I didn't want to be. I didn't know when I would have the conversation with him but it needed to be soon. I didn't want to have another staff member confront me, not that I believed any of them were anywhere as close to being as crazy as Ashley.

I stopped running to sip my water and catch my breath. It had already been twenty minutes and as I stood there trying to make the decision to keep going or not, the choice was made for me. My beeper went off letting me know that I was needed at the hospital. I headed back to my building to shower and change before being on my way.

When I arrived at the hospital and headed up to where Stella was, I could already tell that something was off and when I saw her, she confirmed it.

"Thank God you're here," Stella said as she made her way up to me with a stack of charts in her hand.

"What's happening?" I asked. I looked around the floor and noticed that there weren't as many staff members there as normal and the ones that were there looked overworked.

Stella shook her head. She looked stressed out. "Dr. Cameron is out with the flu, and he took another doctor and two nurses out sick with him so we're short staffed. So, be prepared to be all over."

"The flu? It's the middle of spring," I said in confusion.

"I know," Stella said, "but he just came back from vacation with it and instead of staying home, he brought his ass in here and got *everyone* sick. We're just gonna have to deal for a while. I have to try and adjust some schedules so that we're not completely overwhelmed."

"Damn," I said. "Alright, well, where do you need me?"

"Start off in the clinic and then check in with me," she said. "It's basically just you and whoever is already down there."

"Wouldn't be the first time," I commented before I went on my way.

The day was hectic, to say the least. I worked the clinic as best as I could but there were already more than a few morning appointments, not to mention walk ins. There was only myself and a handful of other doctors down there to handle them all. Most of the people I was seeing weren't even patients of mine but I had their charts so I helped them out.

After dealing with stuff in the clinic, I checked in with Stella just as we'd planned and she gave me another set of charts and told me to start my rounds on the floors. I didn't mind it because she looked just as stressed as I did, maybe even more so.

I was rushing down one of the long hallways of the hospital towards another patient room when I spotted Christian. He'd just stepped off of an elevator and shook someone's hands. He looked like he was about to go one way and turn a corner but stopped when he saw me.

"Kallie," he called out to me as I made my way down the hall. I was in a rush so I planned on just walking passed him. "Do you have a moment?" Christian was dressed in a gray suit and expensive shoes.

I looked down at my watch. "I'm in a hurry, so only if this is quick," I said. I wasn't trying to be rude, but I did have things to do.

"Why haven't you been returning my calls?" he asked. I knew that's what he was going to say before he said it. Guys could be so typical at times.

"Are you serious right now, Christian?" I asked. "You can't be serious right now."

He didn't let me stop him. "You've been acting funny since the fundraiser," he said, and he even had the nerve to pause as if he was waiting for a response. "And what's this I hear about you not claiming me? Telling people that we're just friends and what not. What's going on, Kallie?"

Christian and I were in the middle of the hallway, which worked out in my favor. If I'd have let him pull me into a room or something, it would have given the impression that I had time to deal with him, and I definitely didn't.

"Christian, we can talk about this later," I said. "I have work to do." I turned and started to walk away, headed towards the patient that I was intending on seeing.

"No, we can talk now," he said. As I moved down the hallway, so did he.

"Christian, I have a patient!" I said.

"I can wait," he said persistently. I couldn't believe the nerve of him. I thought about making a call to security to come and get him since he was clearly stopping me from doing my job by harassing me, but I knew that they'd never remove a board member.

Christian followed me all the way to the room that I was going to and I had to remind him that he wasn't allowed to go in with me.

I spent the next ten or fifteen minutes talking to one of my patients, Mr. Walker. He was in his sixties and had just been diagnosed with diabetes. I had to speak with him about what his next steps were and what changes he needed to make to his diet.

When I stepped out of the room, I fully expected for the coast to be clear, but it wasn't.

He was doing something on his cellphone, but Christian was leaned up against the wall. He'd apparently been waiting for me. He put his phone in his pocket when I stepped out of the room. I took a deep breath to try and calm myself down.

"What the hell is wrong with you?" I asked. "I have a job! This isn't a playground. I have patients and responsibilities."

Christian walked passed me towards a room one door over from where I was. He opened the door, grabbed me by the shoulder and steered me inside. He closed the door behind us.

"We need to talk," he repeated himself.

It seemed like he was determined to turn this into a bigger conversation. I knew that he wasn't going to leave me alone until we'd spoken, even if I was at work. All of this was a part of my issue with him; he believed that his time was more important than everyone else's, so when he was ready, everyone else needed to be as well. If he wanted to talk, I'd oblige him, but I wasn't about to make it easy on him.

"Fine," I snapped. "What's on your mind?"

He sighed and shook his head. "I told you before. I don't like what I'm hearing," he said.

"Not to mention that you haven't been hitting me back when I call or text you."

"I've been busy," I said. "I tried to talk to you about all of this but you wouldn't listen."

"I'm listening now," he said.

"And I'm not talking about any of that right now," I countered. I folded my arms across my chest. "But if you wanna talk about something, how's Ashley?"

He got this stupid look on his face. "I don't know," he said. "I told you before that I cut that girl off."

I shook my head at him. When I'd come into the hospital after the fundraiser, people started to treat me differently. However, the only person who'd had the balls to actually confront me had been Ashley and I'd made it clear to her that we were friends. If word of that had gotten back to Christian, it could have only come from her.

"Oh please," I said. "She was the only person that asked me about you instead of just talking behind my back. So if you're out here claiming that *you're* not being claimed, I know who the source is."

Much like any other man who'd been

caught in a lie, I could see the wheels turning quickly on his face. He opened his mouth to speak and then closed it again. He opened it back up, sounding more confident.

"Don't try and change the subject," he said. I shook my head again.

"Stop telling me what to do," I said. "And are you really gonna sit here and try and duck and dodge the statement. You and her are still talking and you've got the nerve to be trying to get me to call you back? I can't believe this shit."

"Calm down," his deep voice rumbled.

"No," I said loudly. I realized then that our conversation was turning into a full-blown argument. "I'm not calming down. You wanted to talk, right? Well I'm talking. Since she's running her mouth, did she tell you about the unprofessional way that she pulled me to the side to talk to me? That bitch is crazy and the two of you deserve one another."

It was Christian's turn to roll his eyes. "I already told you that there's nothing going on with her anymore. We ran into each other and had a quick conversation. That's it."

One thing about me was that I hated for people to play on my intelligence and that's what he was doing. There was no way that my name should have been coming up in a quick and casual conversation between the two of them.

I was just about to keep going, especially since I was upset now but my pager went off. I looked down at it and saw that I was needed in the E.R.

"Look, I have to go," I said. I was about to head towards the door when Christian grabbed my arm. I pulled it loose from his grip.

"You can wait a few more minutes," he said.

"No," I said firmly, "I can't." I wanted to lay into him even more but I needed to go. My pager went off again. This time it was a personal page from Stella herself. She only did that in case of emergencies.

"I'll talk to you later," I said. I stepped passed him and walked out into the hallway before he could say anything else to me.

I stepped off the elevator on the floor that the E.R. was on. Making my way down the hall, I already knew that I was about to have my work cut out for me.

"Kallie!" Stella said as she came up to me. She was in her scrubs and had some blood on her. "Sorry for the double page but we have a situation."

"What is it?" I asked

She looked down at a paper in her hands. "Male, 25 years old and approximately 215 pounds. Multiple bullet wounds to the chest and abdomen. He's in trauma one and needs to be stabilized. It's not looking too good. He's lost a lot of blood."

"I'm on it," I said. No matter what happened, I wasn't about to let this patient die on my watch!

CHAPTER 11

O n my first day of medical school, my professor had given the entire class a lesson and closed it with some advice that she said that we'd remember forever. She said that not everyone in the room would make it into the medical world and that was fine. She said that doctors were special people because they got a chance to do things that normal people would never do on a daily basis. As I stood over my patient, realizing that I'd saved his life, I couldn't help but to have her words come back to me and play over and over in my head. I had saved a life.

Miles Wilson was the name of the patient that I had to stabilize. He'd come into the hospital clinging to his life. His body had been shot full of bullet holes and he'd been covered in blood. In all honesty I didn't know if I'd be able to save him, and I almost didn't. Twice he'd almost died on the operating table. His blood pressure had dropped quickly and suddenly and I had to work hard to get him stable again. The second time was because he was low on blood and I couldn't get to one of the bullets that had been lodged in his body. It had been touch-and-go for a while, but he was stable. It had been a few hours and most of his blood had been replaced. Luckily for him, all the bullets had managed to miss his major organs.

Miles' body was puffy from swelling. He was laying on his back with his hands at his sides as his chest heaved up and down. He wasn't hooked up to a ventilator but we did have him on some oxygen to assist him with his breathing. He had a lot of medication inside of him and it would be hours before he woke up.

While operating on him, I was struck by the fact that he was so young. I knew from his chart that he was only two years older than me but his face just looked so innocent that I couldn't believe someone would do something so crazy to him. He looked like he wouldn't hurt a fly.

I couldn't tell what he really looked like because he'd been unconscious and covered in blood when he came in but he appeared to be handsome. His skin was the color of peanut butter and his short hair was cut low and wavy.

Usually when I came out of such surgeries I was met by the family of the patient. This time around had been different though. It had been almost a full 24 hours and no one had come to see him. No family, no friends, no one. I felt bad for him. I knew that if it were me I would want someone there to check on me. Since no one had come for him, I decided to just be that person for him. I'd been checking in on him periodically since we'd let him out of surgery a few hours ago. I would only stay for a minute or two. He didn't even know I was there because of the medicine he was on.

"Here you are," a voice said behind me. "A nurse told me I'd find you in here."

I turned my head just as Stella stepped into the room. "Hey Stella," I said. "I didn't know you were looking for me. You should have paged me."

"It's alright. I found you now," she said. She turned her head to look at the patient. She walked over to him and looked at the medicine bags that hung next to him. They were pumping fluids and medicine into him to help him heal. "I need your help closing someone up. Nothing too serious, but you're good at that sort of thing."

"No problem," I said.

"I don't wanna sound rude but it's a little creepy to be hanging in a patient's room like this," she said with a smirk. "We have a whole cafeteria downstairs if you wanted some place to chill out."

"No one's come to check on him. Can you believe that?" I asked her as our eyes met. "He's so young. And he came in with all those bullets. How the hell do you think he got caught up in whatever got him shot?"

"It was most likely some stupid gang stuff," Stella brushed it off with a wave of her hand. "You know how a lot of these young guys can be sometimes. They get caught up in a lifestyle that they're not ready for."

I was surprised by Stella's words. "I don't know," I said in disagreement. "I just can't believe it. He doesn't look the type." I looked down at him again.

"Who knows?" Stella said in a dismissive way. "Come on, let me help you scrub up so you can finish the surgery."

"Alright," I said as we headed out of the room.

I finished up the procedure just as Stella had asked me to. A woman was having a small non-cancerous tumor removed from her stomach. It would have been easy but no one could find where she was bleeding from once we were inside, so they asked me to step in and finish it up. I was glad that people were counting on me when it really mattered.

I didn't know what it was about Miles that had him stuck inside my head. Stella always told me that I couldn't get too personal with the patients but I couldn't help it at times. It was just in my nature.

When I got home that night I fell asleep and had a dream. Miles was in it, except he was healthy and unharmed. In the dream he couldn't see me, but I was watching him. My mind was playing games with me and kept showing me all the different ways that he could have gotten shot, each crazier than the one before it. I'd just finished watching Miles rob a bank and he was about to get shot when I woke up.

Buzz.

Buzz.

Groggily I opened my eyes and stretched out my hand to the nightstand. The vibrations of my phone had taken me right out of my dream. I saw that it was Christian calling. I double clicked the button on the side to send it to voice-mail. I turned the vibrations off and rolled over to go back to sleep.

CHAPTER 12

I woke up the following morning feeling refreshed. I had a good night's sleep and was ready for the day. I had to be at work by 10 A.M. but I was aiming on getting there a little earlier. I wanted to check in on Miles and see how he was doing before I got started with my shift.

I'd already laid out my clothes for work and had packed my bag for the day. Since I was already up I decided to go on a run before work instead of after. I threw on my sweatpants and a t-shirt and headed downstairs.

Stepping out of my apartment building and into the fresh air of the morning, I was surprised to find a familiar face just outside of my apartment building. I could tell from the look on his face and his posture that he had been waiting for me.

"Christian?" I stopped and pulled my headphones out of my ear. "What are you doing here? You look like a creep just waiting outside of the building like this."

"I figured that if I went up, you wouldn't have let me in since you've been ducking and dodging my calls," he said. "We need to talk."

Well, so much for my run, I thought to myself. He was right. We did need to talk. Even though I would have liked to have been having the conversation on my own terms, I guessed that it would be best to just get it out of the way then. Last time that we'd tried to talk to one another things had gotten a bit heated and

"Agreed," I said. I looked down at his clothes and he wasn't dressed for running alongside me. "How about we walk and talk?"

"Sure," he said. The two of us set off down the block. We were silent at first. I wasn't planning on starting the conversation since he was the one who'd shown up outside of *my* building.

"What's going on with you, Kallie?" Christian asked. "You've been acting out lately."

"I'm not a child so I'm not "acting out," I said to him with a little attitude. Even his last statement had been a reflection of what pissed me off about him. "I can't mince my words anymore. You're incredibly arrogant and it gets on my nerves."

He didn't deny it or seem the least bit phased by what I said. "How so?"

"You act like you're not only God's gift to women but His gift to me," I said. I took a deep breath and let it out in a huff. "I don't feel like I get a say in what goes on between us and it's annoying. Everything was cool at first but after a while I saw some things that I didn't really like."

"Like what?" Christian asked. I was glad that I seemed to have his full attention this time around. I just hoped that he was actually listening to me and not playing around.

"Like the fact that you want to choose everything we do and everywhere we go. I'm grown. I can make my own decisions," I said. "Not to mention that I shouldn't have to go back and correct your mistakes by telling people that we're together when we're not."

"But you know how I feel about you, right?" Christian asked.

I nodded my head. "I like you, Christian. I think you're a good guy and all but I can't be forced into a relationship. I don't want to feel forced into something that I'm not ready for and you can't make me. If something is gonna happen between us, it needs to be because we sat down and talked about it, not because you decided it was what you wanted and just expected for me to go with it."

Christian nodded his head. "I understand what you're saying," he replied. "I can sometimes get a little ahead of myself, but I don't mean it in a bad way. I guess I'm just used to getting what I want."

"And not taking no for an answer," I added. I was listening to what he was saying and I realized that he hadn't actually said that he was sorry, just that he understood where I was coming from. He probably didn't even see anything wrong with it.

Christian nodded his head. "How about we go out tonight? Nothing too crazy but we can pick some place that you want to go."

I shrugged my shoulders. "I don't know," I said. "I'm not sure if I'm ready to jump into things all over again."

Christian smiled at me, flashing that set of pearly white teeth. "Oh, come on Kallie," he said, "how else am I gonna make it up to you if we don't hang out?"

"I don't know," I said unsurely.

"How about we flip a coin?" He reached into his pocket and pulled out a quarter. "Tails I win, heads you lose."

I couldn't help but to laugh at his silliness. "What? Hell no," I laughed.

Christian stopped walking right in front of me. "I'm not letting you go on your run until you say you're gonna go out with me tonight," he said.

"You know I can just run the other way, right?" I asked.

"If you do that then I'll have to chase you. It won't be too comfortable in my suit but I don't mind. So, what do you say?" Christian was turning on the charm in a big way and it was working on me.

"Fine," I said. "I'll go out with you."

He smiled even brighter. "Good," he said. "I'll let you get back to your run." Christian leaned down a planted a kiss on my cheek before he headed off down the block in the opposite direction.

My run was a little bit shorter since Christian had taken up some of my time. When I got back to my apartment I showered, changed, and headed out the door for work.

I got to the hospital even quicker than I'd planned on. I decided to drive myself into work that day instead of taking a cab and I was glad because the traffic had been lighter than usual. I put my stuff into my locker and checked my watch. I still had a little while before I needed to check in with Stella and start my day so I went upstairs headed towards Miles' room.

When I got to his room it was obvious that someone had been there. There was a small bouquet of flowers and some kind of gift wrapped present next to it. I looked down at the colorful flowers and thought about lifting the present to try and see what it was but I decided against it. I didn't want to be that nosey, especially since I didn't know what it was or who it was from.

I double checked all of the machines next to him and then took a look at his chart. Everything appeared to be going normally for him. It had only been about a day since he'd come out of surgery but he looked a little better. There was color returning to his skin and some of the swelling had gone down. According to his charts they'd decreased his meds just a little bit but he still hadn't woken up.

I left his room a few minutes later and went ahead and got started with my shift. I took care of my duties like I was supposed to, glad that I had come in early so I had more time to prepare for my day.

My lunch came quickly which I was glad for. I headed downstairs and grabbed something from the cafeteria and ate it. Afterwards I headed back upstairs to check in on Miles again. This time when I walked into the room, someone else was there.

"Hey Dr. Jameson," said Olivia, one of the nurses on the floor. She was in the room on her rounds, changing out an IV bag in Miles' room.

"Hey Olivia, how are you?" I asked. I hadn't planned on running into anyone else in his room, not that I was hiding or anything.

"I'm alright. Almost time for me to head out," she said with a smile before turning her head towards Miles. Olivia was an older woman with a motherly personality. "Do you know him? I've seen you up here a few times since he's been out of surgery. You did a good job by the way. I heard he came in in real rough shape."

"Thanks," I said. "He did. He was all kinds of banged up. And no, I don't know him. It's just…"

"It's alright. I already know," she said with a knowing smirk. "He looks like a baby, which makes everybody wanna take care of him."

I smiled at her. "Exactly," I said. "I just can't believe that he's been in here alone for so long. Did you happen to see who came to visit him? They left the flowers and the gift I'm assuming."

Olivia shook her head. "I wasn't around when they brought all this stuff in," she said, waving her hands at the flowers. "I would probably assume that it was the same guys who came in last night to see him."

I raised my eyebrows in surprise. "Guys? Who were they?" She'd definitely piqued my curiosity.

"I don't know," she said with a shrug. "But they seemed to be nice enough young men. They didn't come in making a scene or anything especially since it was late. They sat in the room with him and read him Bible verses. He didn't wake up, but they seemed confident that he'd heard them."

I wasn't expecting that response at all. I didn't know anything about Miles, but the mystery surrounding him only seemed to be growing in my head. I assumed that the people that had come to visit him were most likely family members, but who know what the truth really was?

"Wow," I said. "Did they say anything to anyone?"

"No," she said with another nod of her head. "They asked for him by another name."

"Another name?" I screwed my face up in confusion. I'd looked at his chart a bunch of times so I knew what his name was. "What name?"

Olivia took a step closer to me and spoke in a low tone like she was afraid someone would hear her, even though the only other person in the room was unconscious. "Well, there's something funny about this one."

"Funny how?" I asked.

"The name on his charts is the right one. It's pulled straight off of his ID, but he's here under a fake name: James K. Williams," she explained. I opened my mouth to ask what she meant but she kept right on going. "He must be someone pretty important to be keeping secrets like this. Not a lot of people in the hospital know his name is actually Miles and if I were you I'd keep that to myself. Something tells me that there's more to this one than meets the eye."

Olivia walked out of the room after that, most likely headed towards her next patient. I stayed inside and walked a little closer to Miles. I ran my hand over his bandaged chest.

"So, who are you? Miles or James?" I asked out loud as I looked down at his sleeping face. It was interesting to me that all of this was happening. It wasn't the first time that someone had come into the hospital under an assumed name but those people were usually celebrities trying to hide something. He didn't seem to be any kind of famous person that I knew. I also knew that the hospital wouldn't give anyone that kind of anonymity unless they demanded it and were willing to pay the extra costs.

I left the room soon after and headed back on duty. I was working a long 12 hour shift that day and it had definitely taken its toll on me. I wanted to get home and take a long bath. I had some white wine in the fridge that I was planning on enjoying too.

Before I left, I decided to check on Miles again. I knew that I was doing the most by stopping in on him but Olivia's words earlier had really sent my mind going. I knew it wasn't my job to try and figure him out but there was definitely a lot more to him than I'd initially thought.

I headed into the room and stood in front of the chair closest to his bed. He was still unconscious, but I knew that he would most likely be waking up sometime soon since they'd been decreasing his medication. It wasn't too late, but I was wondering if the guys who'd come to visit him before would be coming back again.

I was snapped from my thought when I thought I saw something move under the covers close to Miles' feet. I stared at them for a full minute waiting for them to move again but they didn't do it again. I thought for sure that I'd imagined it but then I heard a sound which made me jump.

"Ugh," Miles moaned a long and hollow sound that sounded somewhere between pain and sleep. His head turned a little bit as he let the sound out of him.

He was waking up. As if to confirm it, the monitor by his bedside started to beep. His heartbeat was increasing and his blood pressure was rising quickly. A nurse came into the room a few seconds later.

"Dr. Jameson?" asked a nurse name Sharice. She was fairly new and I hadn't worked with her too much but I heard she had a way with the patients that was great. "What's happening?"

"He's waking up," I said as I double checked the machines next to him. Miles still hadn't opened his eyes but his hands and feet were moving as if he was trying to figure out how to use them again. "Get me a new morphine bag and a mild sedative. He's gonna need it once he's fully awake and realizes what's going on. And call his family."

Sharice looked like she wanted to ask why I was in the room but she just nodded her head and walked out of the room to get the medicine.

Miles' hazel colored eyes burst open widely. He looked around in shock, trying to take in everything around him. I had seen more than a handful of patients come out of something like this and it was always a shock. They wake up scared and trying to panic.

"Wha—" Miles tried to speak but his throat must have been dry from not using his voice for so long. He closed it and tried to swallow. He put his hands on the railings on the side of the bed to try and pull himself up but he winced in pain.

"Mr. Wilson," I said in a calming voice as I put my hand on top of his to try and calm him down, "you're safe. You're in a hospital. You've been shot and I had to save your life."

He didn't look any less concerned, so I tried a trick that I'd picked up. I leaned down and got close to his ear. "You're gonna be alright. You are alive and well but you have to calm down."

He seemed to relax just a little bit then. I stood back up right on time. Three guys came in with concerned looks on their faces. I didn't know them but I assumed that they were the same guys who'd come in the other night and prayed for him.

Nurse Sharice came back into the room with a cup of water and holding two bags of medicine. She handed the small white cup to Miles who drank the whole thing down in one gulp and tried to hand it back to Sharice. She and I were busy getting his medicine set up.

"Fuck! This a lot of pain!" Miles finally spoke and his voice was raspy and deep. I could tell that his throat was dry.

I decided that it was my chance to make my exit. I excused myself from the room just as the guys who had come in went and huddled next to Miles. I took one last look before I made my way out of the room and headed home.

CHAPTER 13

The following day I was out getting coffee with Stella on our lunch break. The day had been incredibly busy so I had insisted that we go and get something from somewhere outside of the hospital. There were some days where I went in before the sun came up and didn't leave until after it had already gone down. It was sad, but on some days I really had to remind myself that it was alright for me to go out.

I hadn't had a chance to check in Miles that day because of how busy it was. If things kept going the way that they were, I wouldn't have a chance to see him during my shift at all. I was a little upset about it but pushed it out of my mind as I listened to Stella.

We were seated in the back of the coffee shop that we usually went to. The small table was in a back corner close to the bathrooms. Stella had gotten a sandwich and I was drinking my second coffee of the day. I needed the energy.

"And then when we got to my house, that was it," Stella said with her eyes closed like she was having a flashback. "I thought the stuff in the back of the car was good but *baby*, when I tell you that he really put it on me!"

Stella had been talking for the last few minutes. She'd been going on and on about some guy that she'd hooked up with that had really put it on her. I was halfway listening to her. No shade but Stella had sex so damn often that all the stories seemed to blend into one really long sexual escapade.

"Was it good?" I asked. I tried not to stay silent so she knew I was paying attention.

She got a confused look on her face. "Good? Good ain't the word for what it was. I like this one. I might have to keep him around, just for the dick."

"I hear that," I said.

"How are things with you and Christian?" she asked as she took a sip of her coffee. "You guys went out the other night, right?"

I nodded my head. "Yeah, we did."

"So why do you sound so blah about it?" Stella asked.

I half-heartedly shrugged. "There's not really much to tell," I said. "We had some dinner at his condo. It was my first time there."

"Was it nice?" Stella asked curiously.

"Yeah, really nice," I said with a nod. "I don't know who decorated it but they did a good job. Big and spacious with two bedrooms and more rooms that I didn't see."

"That sounds nice," Stella said. "I'm sure his family home is nice too. So, what happened?'

"Nothing really," I said. "We ate the food and chilled out. I ended up staying the night but…"

"But what?" She asked.

"I don't know," I said. "I just didn't feel comfortable being there. I spent the night but couldn't 't really sleep. I just wanted to be back in my house. The vibe was just off."

"So what's wrong with Christian?" Stella

asked. "You two have been dealing with each other for a while now but you don't seem to be going anywhere."

I took a long breath and let it out slowly. "I just...his personality," I struggled to find the words. "Christian can just be a dick sometimes. He doesn't apologize. He doesn't admit when he's wrong. He tries to control everything. You know I'm not with that at all."

"Have you tried talking to him about it?" Stella asked.

"Yeah, a bunch of times," I admitted. "But it just goes in one ear and comes out the other. It's like he just tells me what I want to hear and then he moves on and tries to have sex or something. It's annoying."

"Are you sure that you're not blowing it out of proportion?" Stella asked. "Don't get me wrong. You're with him and I'm not, so of course you have the inside scoop and everything. But I also know from experience how hard it can be to transition from being single for a long time into a relationship or even seriously dating someone."

It took me a few seconds to respond as I thought about what she was saying. I knew that

Christian could be a lot but was there a chance
that I was doing too much? He could be controlling at times and I just didn't want to think
about it. The more that I thought, the more I
realized that I wasn't taking it out of context. If
things between Christian and I went ahead and
got serious, there was every chance that things
would get even worse as far as him controlling
me went.

Stella and I finished up our conversation
and headed back to the hospital. I was on my
way back to the nurse's station that I was
working from when I decided to take a couple
of minutes to go check on Miles. I headed
upstairs to his room. I saw that there was a
nurse inside the room, so I waited until she left
before I went in.

I walked into the room and saw that Miles
was awake. He was laying down in his bed.
From what I heard, he hadn't been up and
walking or even sitting up without assistance yet.
I knew he would get there eventually though.
His entire body tensed up when he saw me but
relaxed as he looked down at my clothes and
saw that I was a doctor.

"I'm sorry. I didn't mean to startle you," I said. "I should have knocked."

"Are you my doctor?" He looked at my chest searching for my name tag. "Dr. Jameson? That's you?" His eyes got wide. "I was expecting someone else."

I pulled my badge from my pocket and pinned it to my chest. "Yeah, that's me."

Miles' eyes were intent as they followed me across the room. I was headed to check on his IV and medicine bags and to look at his charts. I wasn't looking at him but I could feel his eyes on me.

"Did I scare you?" I asked as I turned back to him and looked him in his light eyes.

"Nah, not at all," he said. "But I was just surprised that someone walked so boldly into my room like that. Thank you for saving my life."

I was blushing after he said that and I couldn't figure out why. It wasn't the first time that a patient thanked me. Sometimes they even hugged me or something like that. Doing what I did for Miles was nothing out of the ordinary for me but I couldn't figure out why he was the one that had stuck with me the most.

"It's alright. You don't have to thank me. I was just doing my job," I said. I hated how cliché that sounded, but it was the truth. "You just make sure that you get yourself better so that you don't end up in here again. I don't know what happened, but it wasn't anything good.

"I'll try, but I can't make any promises," he said. I couldn't tell if he was being serious or not. Miles tried to sit up but he ended up wincing in pain.

I put my hand on his shoulder. "You have to take it slow," I said. "You're really banged up."

I got closer to him and helped him set himself up. Our eyes locked and I realized then how handsome he was. The swelling on his face and body that had been horrible before had finally gone down a lot. His lips were full and his low eyes were bright and serious. He had a strong jawline and a bunch of tattoos all over his body.

Our eyes stayed locked on one another until I heard a noise coming from behind us which caused me to take a step back from the bed. The guys who'd come into the room when he was waking up had returned. There were three of them. One guy was really tall and the others were average height.

"Fellas, this is my doctor, the woman who saved my life, Dr. Jameson," Miles made the introduction. "Dr. James, these are some of my boys."

"Nice to meet you," I said with a friendly smile. I turned back to Miles. "I'll let you and your friends visit. I'll be back to check on you a little later on. Take it easy in the meantime."

I left and headed home not too long afterwards. I was glad for it too. The day had been long and tiring.

I thought about stopping and grabbing a bottle of wine but decided against it. I sat up in bed watching the television for a little bit before I finally drifted off to sleep. I thought that since I was so tired that I might just sleep through the night, but it seemed that someone had other plans for me.

I woke up in the middle of the night. My breathing was heavy. My sweaty body was wrapped up in the sheets that I'd used to cover me. I looked over at my phone to see that it was a little after one o'clock in the morning.

I'd had a dream...almost like a fantasy. Miles

was in it. He didn't look the way that he did in the hospital. I had never seen him before he showed up with the bullet holes in him but in the dream he looked the way that I'd imagined him to be when he was back on his feet for real; sexy as hell. I couldn't remember every part of the dream but the parts that I could remember had done enough to me that my body was craving the real thing.

I only thought about it for a few seconds before I grabbed my phone. I knew that there was one person I could call that could put out the fire that the dream had started. I sent a quick *"Are you up?"* text and waited a full minute for a response. I thought for a little bit that I might have to take care of myself so I was happy when my phone lit up letting me know that Christian had text me back.

Christian showed up at my house within half an hour. He was wearing a pair of gray sweatpants and a black t-shirt. When he came inside the house he tried to start a little conversation but once he saw me drop my robe, it was on.

For the next hour, Christian was mine. The sex that we had was beyond amazing. At a certain point, even he had to take a minute to ask me what had gotten into me because I was acting really sexual. He wasn't complaining though. I didn't even let him take me into the bedroom. I knew that it was risky, but we had sex right in front of my floor length windows in the living room. I thought about going to the balcony but that was way too risky. I rode the hell out of him right there on the floor and when I was done, I collapsed on top of him, breathing like I'd just run a marathon.

Christian and I couldn't even make it to the bedroom. The two of us fell asleep right there on the floor with a sheet loosely draped over the two of us. No more than a minute or two after we finished, he was knocked out and snoring lightly next to me. I rolled over and laid my arm across his chest. He'd really put in work. The thing that was bugging me was that all of this had been inspired by Miles.

CHAPTER 14

The following morning, Christian and I woke up and got dressed for work. He needed to head back to his condo before he headed in, but he asked me if I needed a ride. I declined, letting him know that I'd call him whenever I got a chance. He tried to be a little sentimental and give me a long goodbye kiss but I cut it short and let him know that I was in a rush. I didn't tell him that I wanted to be in a little earlier so I could check on Miles.

I got dressed and made it to work a lot quicker than I'd expected. I was glad that there hadn't been any traffic. Since I had more than enough time to spare, I headed straight for

Miles' room after I dropped my stuff off at my locker.

His room door was open but I still knocked on it before I stepped all the way inside. Miles was sitting up in his bed. I saw that though the bed itself was elevated, he was supporting his own weight which was a good sign. I knew that sometimes after surgeries the pain could stop people from wanting to move too much.

"Good morning," I said with a smile. "I see that you're sitting up on your own." I walked over to the floor of the bed and crossed my arms over my chest.

"Morning," he said with a smile on his face thanks to my compliment. "It still hurts but I gotta start working on it."

"I know how that can be," I said. "I've seen a lot of patients go through similar surgeries but they usually wait a while before they try and sit up."

"Well, I'm not like other patients," he said with a smirk.

"I can see that," I said in a way that was unintentionally flirtatious. "I'm proud of your progress. I'm sure that you'll be up and walking around again in no times. Just make sure to keep those legs moving as much as you can."

"That won't be a problem," he said. His eyes glanced down at my body before he looked me in the eyes, not even trying to hide it. "I see that you keep your legs moving too. Do you run?"

"At least once a day," I said.

"I can tell," he said. He was flirting with me for sure. I opened my mouth to say something else but was stopped when there was another knock at the door. One of the orderlies was bringing around the breakfast tray. He said his good mornings and got the roll around table set up. He plopped a pink tray with a lid on it down in front of Miles and left the room.

Miles looked down at the tray expectantly and then took the lid off. I couldn't help but to laugh when I saw his whole body deflate when he saw the sad looking meal on the plate in front of him. There was a sad looking pile of eggs and two sausage links next to it. They'd also given him two pieces of whole wheat toast and a small fruit salad. I had to admit that it didn't look appetizing, or even filling for that matter.

"You should see your face right now," I said as I tried to hide my laughter.

"What am I supposed to do with this?" He looked up at me with disbelief. "First of all, this food don't even look cooked." He put his hand out over the food. "And it's not even hot. It's barely warm."

"I know it doesn't look good but you can't handle too much right now," I explained. "You're still on a lot of medications and your diet has to be made for you to handle it."

"Ugh," he said, closing his eyes and pushing the plate away from him. "What I wouldn't give for some real food right now." His eyes popped open and he looked at me. "Dr. Jameson, could you...?"

"No," I said with a shake of my head. "I just said that your diet is especially for you."

He was determined. "Oh, come on," he pleaded. "I don't want anything crazy. I'm not asking for a bacon, egg and cheese or something crazy. I just want something edible. You see this. I can't eat this." He held up his sorry looking plate.

"I can't," I said, shaking my head again. "Besides, where would I even get food from?"

"The hospital has a cafeteria," he said. "It doesn't even have to be anything fancy."

I took a deep breath and dropped my arms to my side. "I see you're not gonna let this go," I said.

"I'm really determined when I know what I want," he said.

"Fine," I said as I checked the time on my phone. "But it won't be right now. I've got to go and get my day started. I'll see you in a little bit. And this has to stay between us, alright?"

"Not a problem," he said with a nod of his head. "I'm good at keeping secrets."

"See you in a few," I said.

I went upstairs and checked in with Stella. I didn't mention anything about Miles to her. I didn't know what she would think about the situation and I wasn't in the mood to find out either. I knew that I wasn't using the best judgement in the situation with Miles but I at least planned on being cautious about it.

I went ahead and did my rounds as quickly as I could. I saw three patients before I decided that the coast was clear for me. I headed down to the hospital's cafeteria and looked around for some stuff that I could bring Miles. I finally decided to get him some fruit, a croissant sandwich, and some orange juice. Everything was small enough that I didn't have any problems putting it all into my lab coat and heading back up to his room.

I headed back up to his room and when I got inside I closed the door behind me. I pulled the food out of my pockets and handed it to him. Everything was wrapped in plastic so it was clean.

"Here you go," I said. "I had to make sure it was something healthy."

Miles looked down at the food and I saw his eyes light up. "Damn, this sandwich looks good," he said. He grabbed my hand dramatically and started to kiss it. "Thanks so much, doc. I appreciate it."

"No problem," I said. I thought about snatching my hand back but his big hands just felt so nice.

"I mean it," he said with a smile as he started to unwrap the food. "You're beautiful, smart, and a rider. Not too many people would have done this for me."

I finally took my hand back him, slowly and gently. "Wow, all of this for a sandwich and some fruit. I'd hate to see what you do for dinner."

"Maybe you'll find out one day," he said flirtatiously. His words hung in the air with an almost awkward silence.

I didn't know how to respond so I gave Miles a few minutes to eat his food. When he finished, he wiped his mouth and turned to me.

"Thanks again," he said. "I mean it."

"Not a problem," I said. "I'm sure someone else would have done it for you if they'd come to visit."

He shook his head. "Maybe," he said, "but everybody isn't you. So, tell me more about yourself. You keep coming up here and we don't really talk about much."

"What do you wanna know?" I asked.

"Well, and I don't want you to take offense to this, but are you single? I only ask cause you seem like you have a good head on your shoulders. Somebody should have scooped you up by now."

I nodded my head. "I'm single…" I said and my voice trailed off.

"I can see a "but" on your face," Miles said.

"I guess I'm trying to work through something with someone right now," I admitted. "It's complicated."

Miles nodded his head with understanding. "Yeah, I know how that goes. I've been in my fair share of complicated situations."

I didn't want it to turn into a situation about Christian and I so I decided to ask my own questions. "What about you? I haven't seen a girlfriend or baby mother come in here to visit you. Are you single?"

Miles nodded his head slowly. "Yeah," he said. "Single with no kids."

"Why not?" I asked. "You seem like a good guy," I returned his compliment.

Miles hesitated for just a few seconds but it was long enough for me to notice. "My line of work won't let me get close to too many people, especially women," he said.

There were a lot of different ways that I could take that response but I just frowned and stayed silent instead of pressing him for more details.

Miles and I chopped it up for a few more minutes before I told him that I needed to get back to my own floor to do some work. I was at the door about to leave when Miles called out to me.

"Yo, Doc...Kallie," he said my name, and I liked the way it sounded coming from him.

"Yeah?" I turned around and walked back over to him.

"I just..." he started but searched for the words to say, "I just wanted to say that I like when you come around. It's the best part of my day."

I immediately felt myself starting to blush. "It's no problem. It's a part of my job," I said, modestly.

Miles shook his head. "Nah, I mean it," he said. His bright hazel eyes were staring deeply into mine. "I don't know what people in this hospital think of me, but you don't treat me like what everybody thinks I am. You talk to me like a real person and where I'm from, I don't get that often. I've seen a lot of women but none of them have been as well put together as you. You're classy and I can tell you really care about what you do. I like your passion. I like your determination to be the best. I like talking to you."

It took me a second or two to finally open my mouth. I hadn't been expecting a response like that from him. I knew that he knew that I cared about him in a real way but I wasn't sure of what was happening.

"It's...the best part of my day too," I said slowly. The words sounded strange coming out of my mouth. It briefly crossed my mind that if things kept going the way that they were, we'd soon be blurring the lines between doctor and patient. "I'll see you later."

As I walked out of the room, I could feel his eyes on me.

CHAPTER 15

I couldn't get Miles off of my mind after our conversation. I was making sure to be careful about what I was doing but I started heading up to his room more and more often. I wondered what other people on the floor might have been thinking but I pushed it out of my mind. I knew that I was giving him special treatment but he *was* still a patient of mine which meant that it was my job to check on him.

What was only supposed to be a one-time thing had turned into something more. The next time that I was around when Miles was getting his food, his put on the same song and dance routine and begged me to get him food.

From then on, I tried to being him healthy snacks a few times a day. It was nothing too much, a sandwich or piece of fruit here or there. I knew that he could have probably asked the guys who still came to visit him to bring him stuff but I think he liked giving me a reason to check in on him.

One thing that I'd quickly discovered about Miles was that he was a good listener. He had a real ear for detail and remembered stuff that I said which I liked. I hated talking to someone only to find out later on that they actually weren't paying attention. One night I was up in his room after my shift was over. It was my first time stopping in for the day because I had been busy. I didn't want to leave without saying hello.

When I walked into the room, he was sitting up in his bed watching one of those cop shows that always seemed to be on. He smiled when he saw me and sat up to turn the TV off.

"You don't have to do all that," I said as I walked over to his bed and grabbed his chart. "I just wanted to pop in on you before I left for the day."

"So you weren't planning on staying?" Miles

asked in his deep voice with just a hint of disap-
pointment.

I looked down at my watch and then put the
chart back down in the holder at the foot of the
bed. "Fine, just a couple of minutes," I said with
a sigh.

"Cool," he said with a smile. "So, how was
your day?"

"It was good. Long, but good. What about
yours?" I asked. I looked down at his partially
exposed chest to see it was covered in tattoos but
the bandages that he was wearing looked neat
and clean.

"Everyone says I'm healing up well," he
said. "So that's good. I just wish I could get out
of here."

"You've still got a ways to go. Have the physical therapy people been by yet? I know we
discussed you trying to walk," I said.

Miles shook his head with a smirk on his
face. "Ok, so how about we don't talk about
medical stuff? Ain't you off the clock? You gotta
know how to let loose."

"I can't help it. It's in my nature," I said with
a smile. "I've always been the type to help
people."

"Tell me about that," he said in a way that made him sound like a psychiatrist.

"What you wanna know?" I asked.

"What makes you wanna help people so much? It's cool that you do that. I guess I've always just felt that stuff like that is a calling. You know, being a teacher or doctor, somebody like that. You gotta have a good heart," Miles said.

"Well, I grew up on the Southside and I—"

"Wait, *you* grew up on the Southside?" Miles interrupted with surprise all over his face. His eyes had gotten so wide and his eyebrows almost touched his hairline as his face scrunched up. "Like, of Chicago?"

I rolled my eyes. "Of course," I said. "Where else is there? Is that where you're from?"

"Yeah," he said. "I don't live there no more but you know everybody still has people over there."

"Yeah, I know how that is," I said. "My family isn't too close though so we don't really speak too often."

"I know how family can be. I basically had to take care of myself," Miles said.

"Me too," I said. "Where was your family at?"

"Typical shit," he said as he shrugged. "Pops wasn't around. My mother had other shit to to worry about so when I got old enough to help myself, I did. I've been doing it ever sense."

"You sound like me," I said. I walked over to the chair closest to the bed and took a seat. "People don't know what it's like when you don't feel like you have a support system. I know a lot of people probably look at me like I'm some kind of success story but I'm not. I just realized early in life that if I didn't help myself, I wasn't gonna get helped."

"That's facts," Miles said. "The good thing is that we got out though."

"I agree," I said with a nod of my head. "And we seem to be doing pretty well for ourselves."

"Word," Miles said.

We'd talked more than a few times and Miles had always seemed to skirt over whatever it was he did for a living. I knew that whatever it was it had to be lucrative.

Once Miles was up and about for real, I started noticing new things in his room. The dresser next to his bed had the top drawer open and it was full of designer clothes. On top of the dresser he even had designer toiletries. The biggest surprise had come the day before when I told him that if I didn't know any better, I'd have assumed that he had a haircut since his lineup was so fresh. He informed me that he'd had a barber come in a give him a shape up right there in the room. I couldn't figure Miles out, but I was entertained by the mystery.

One night I finally admitted to myself that I was indeed crushing on him. I knew that it probably wasn't for the best but I just couldn't help it. I knew that I wanted to get a chance to know him better.

Stella and I had plans to go out for a drink one night after work. I asked her if we were going out or *out* out. It meant the difference between me wearing what I wore to work or bringing a change of clothes. She said that she just wanted to have a drink and catch up so whatever I wore was fine.

We headed to a spot a couple of blocks away from the hospital. It was a nice restaurant and bar that had played good music. It was a nice after work spot to hang out at because it didn't get too rowdy.

Stella and I got a table and ordered a round of drinks. We'd had some small talk but nothing too major. I could tell that something was on her mind but I wasn't sure of what. After the drinks arrived she took a couple of sips which seemed to help her open her mouth a little more.

"Are you alright?" I asked her. "You seem like something is on your mind."

"There is," Stella said. She took a deep breath and looked me in the eyes. "Kallie, I want you to be honest with me."

I sat up a little straighter. Stella wasn't one for the dramatics so I figured that whatever she wanted to talk to me about had to be serious. I ran through my mind about anything that I'd been doing lately but couldn't think of a particular thing that would warrant all of this.

"Alright," I said as I took a sip of my drink, "what's up?"

"Miles," Stella said. "What's going on with you and Miles? And before you say nothing, remember who you're talking to."

"I...I just..." I was fumbling trying to find

the right words to say. "I know what it looks like."

"It looks like you have a crush on him," Stella said.

I slowly nodded my head and avoided her eye contact. "Yeah...I guess it does."

"This isn't like you, Kallie," Stella said. "I'd expect this from someone else but not you. How did you end up involved with a patient?"

"We're not 'involved,'" I said as I used air quotes. "We just...have a connection. I can't explain it."

Stella took another sip of her drink and let out a breath. "You gotta do better than that."

"What can I say?" I asked with a shrug. "He's a really nice guy. He's sweet and attentive. He compliments me and makes me feel like his equal. We have a lot in common. We talk about things. If I'd met him under different circumstances I would have given him a chance."

"I can't believe I'm hearing this," Stella said. She frowned.

"I know it's totally out of my character, but it's not like it's something that I planned on doing. It started small and now it's kind of snowballing," I said. I wished that I could have given her a better explanation but what was happening with Miles was so new for me that I couldn't really put it into words. We were really building a connection with one another.

Stella shook her head. "I just want you to be careful. I hear what you're saying about meeting him under different circumstances but you need to remember the *actual* way you met him. He came into our hospital and is under our care because he'd been shot multiple times."

"But we don't know what happened," I tried to argue back.

"Kallie, don't play dumb. You know you're really smart. A man like that with all those tattoos and the mysterious men coming to see him. Not to mention that he's there under and assumed name. He's either hiding from trouble or he's the trouble himself," she explained.

I kept a straight face and listened. I knew that Stella had to be in a difficult position. She was my friend and my boss after all. I knew that she had my best interests in mind and only wanted me to be careful. "I hear you," I said.

"Look, I'm sorry for going so hard but I don't want this whole thing to blow up in your face. At least just try and wait until he's out of the hospital before you take things further. At least then that way you're covered," Stella said.

"I will," I said. I took another sip of my drink and sat back in the chair. I was glad that I'd survived the hot seat this round but I knew that it was only a matter of time before someone brought it up again.

Over the next few days, Miles hit a milestone when he started walking. It was a slow process. When teaching someone to walk again, other factors came into play. The person's age mattered, as well as how long they'd been off their feet, not to mention the condition of their legs. Thankfully for Miles he'd only gotten hit in one leg and though it was sore, he wasn't really facing too many problems as long as he stuck with the routine that had been provided for him.

Miles had been practicing his walking but still needed a nurse to be by him to help him out. I knew it was frustrating to him but he was making progress better than we'd hoped for.

I was of course still checking in on Miles to see how he was doing and to talk with him. On my breaks I'd head into his room and try to help him walk. He tried to argue with me about it at first, claiming that he didn't need want me wasting time on my breaks helping him out, but once I made it clear that it was my choice and not his, he relented.

The hospital had a beautiful and spacious rooftop that they'd had set up so patients could sometimes head up there, as long as they were supervised. It was a beautiful day outside so I decided to take Miles up there for him to walk around some. Plus I knew that he hadn't been outside since he'd been a patient, so the fresh air might have done him so good.

The two of us walked slowly next to one another. He was wearing a white t-shirt and a pair of sweatpants, courtesy of the guys who kept bringing him clothes. On his feet he had on a pair of sneakers. He looked pretty normal except for the walker and the way he moved while he used it.

"Damn, you were right," Miles said. "It is a really nice day outside."

"Yeah it is. I thought it would be nice to come up here and get away," I said. "The hospital has events and stuff up here sometimes but for the most part it's just for the patients to come and relax."

Miles shook his head and looked down at his

walker. "I'm tired of relaxing. I just wanna be able to walk again."

"Don't get frustrated," I said. "I've seen a lot of people make that mistake and then get annoyed with themselves later on when they don't live up to their own expectations."

"Whatever," Miles mumbled. He took another step forward and then another. I could see the look of pain on his face but he was determined not to let it come out of his mouth. The two of us made our way over to one of the benches and had a seat next to one another.

"How's your day going?" Miles asked.

I shook my head with a smirk. "No, how's *your* day going? You ask me that every day like the answer changes. Busy, always busy. Unless I'm not here."

Miles laughed. "Shit, mine is the same too, at least in here. I lay in a bed. I sit up or I walk around," he said. "And my people came to visit me today. They dropped off some more stuff."

"More stuff? You must have the most extensive wardrobe in the hospital," I said with a laugh.

"Oh please," he laughed too.

A thought crossed my mind and I figured it

would be the right time to ask the question that had been on my mind for a while. "I don't wanna be all up in your business or anything, but who are those guys that come and visit you? They're always bringing you stuff."

Miles was facing forward and staring off into the distance but I could see his jaw tighten up when I asked. "They're just friends of mine," he said.

I waited for a couple of seconds to see if he had more to add on but when he didn't I just kept on going. I wasn't trying to pry too much but I realized that there were certain parts of himself that he just kept to himself.

"Oh, ok," I said. "I'm not trying to be nosey. I was thinking they might have been people from your job. What did you say you did for a living again? Must be something nice cause you've got expensive taste." I threw in a laugh at the end to make it sound more conversational, but I was trying to pick his brain.

I could see the uneasiness in his face as he turned to me. "I didn't say," he said. Miles cleared his throat a little bit. "We should probably head back downstairs. Ain't your break almost over?"

Before I could open my mouth to agree or disagree, Miles had already stood back up. He turned to me expectantly before he headed off in the direction of the elevator with me behind him.

I got up and followed behind him. The two of us made our way back downstairs to his room but outside of a couple of words here and there, we hadn't said much to one another. I hoped that I hadn't offended him with my questions.

Once Miles was back on the side of his bed sitting down, I figured it would probably be best to just leave him alone for a while.

"Hey, I'm sorry if I got on your nerves upstairs. I was just trying to make conversation," I said. "I'm gonna head out."

"Hold up," Miles called to me as I got to the door. "It's not your fault. I'm just a little tired, even though I know I'm not gonna sleep like that tonight."

"What's so special about tonight?" I asked.

"Nothing. I just mean that I don't really get good sleep when I'm here. This bed ain't the best, especially not for someone built like me. I need a real bed," he explained.

"Yeah, the mattresses are better than they

were before but as far as space there is none," I
said.

"Um...I was thinking," Miles said in a shy
way, "and you don't have to say yes. But would it
be alright for us to exchange numbers? I got my
cellphone with me now and since I can't sleep,
it'd be nice to have someone to talk to."

We were playing with fire. I knew it. I was
already doing too much as far as things with
Miles and I were concerned. The thing was that
even though I already knew that, I still agreed to
give him my number.

Later that night I was at my apartment
packing a bag. I was heading over to Christians
condo so the two of us could hangout for a little
bit. It was already late so it just made sense for
me to spend the night. I'd already packed my
clothes and just needed to grab my sneakers but
as I was grabbing them, my cell phone went off.
I assumed that it was Christian asking me when
I was leaving but I was surprised to see that it
was Miles.

You know how you can get sidetracked and
forget you were doing something else? That
happened to me. I sat down on the edge of my
bed, cell phone in hand, only intending on

letting Miles know that I'd hit him up later. However, we ended up texting about why he couldn't sleep which then led to a whole other conversation. Before I knew it, I was laid back on the bed with one foot hanging off of it, feeling like a schoolgirl texting her crush.

I genuinely had not expected to get so caught up in the conversation. I was so caught up that before I knew it, an hour and a half had gone by without me noticing. I probably wouldn't have noticed then either if not for Christian texting me asking me was I still coming.

"Oh shit," I said as I looked at the time on my phone. I quickly sent Christian a text apologizing and letting him know that I'd fallen asleep. I told him that I could still come if he wanted.

No. Just stay home if you're that tired. That was Christian's reply. I knew he had to be annoyed with me but I did have every intention of making it over to his place that night. I'd just gotten so caught up in talking to Miles.

Once I knew for sure that I wasn't heading over to Christian's house, I got up and took my clothes off and climbed into bed the right way. I knew it was late but I decided to call Miles on the phone instead of continuing to text him.

I wasn't sure of what time we fell asleep but I do know that just like I had to do in high school, I woke up in the middle of the night to hang the phone up since we'd fallen asleep talking to one another. I knew it was bad, but Miles was giving me butterflies and making me feel things that I hadn't felt in a while.

CHAPTER 16

I felt groggy when I woke up the next morning but I powered through it and still made it to work on time. I knew that spending so much time staying up and talking to Miles was going to hit me hard. I yawned as I walked into the building and then again as I stepped off the elevator.

I was walking passed the desk on the floor when one of the nurses flagged me over. She was on the phone with someone but when I got to her she reached under her desk and grabbed a big bouquet of flowers. I would have asked questions but she was busy helping someone and there was a card. I thanked her and walked away headed towards the locker room.

The bouquet was beautiful. It wasn't just one of those simple premade ones either. Someone had taken time and chosen some really beautiful flowers. I wasn't sure of who could have brought them. My first might have been Christian but I'd cancelled on him the night before so I didn't think he'd be sending me gifts for that.

I took the card from the top and opened it. I was expecting there to be small note telling me who it was from but instead there was a poem written on it.

If there was ever a way for me to thank you
For all the things you've done
I'd do it over and over again
Cause to me you're a special one

I read and reread the short but sweet poem. It was a little cheesy, but I actually liked that kind of stuff.

I headed into the locker room to drop my stuff off. I was putting on my lab coat as I stepped out of the room and noticed the door opening across from me. It looked like a meeting had just let out. I would have moved on but when I saw Christian he smiled brightly when he saw me.

"What's up, Kallie?" Christian asked as he greeted me. I was glad that he hadn't tried to hug me with so many people around.

"I'm good. I see you're in a good mood," I said.

"Why wouldn't I be?" he asked. "So how are you feeling after last night? I know you said you were tired."

"I'm good. Especially after your pick me up," I said.

There was a brief look of confusion on his face. "Pick me up?"

"Yeah," I said with a nod, "the flowers that you got for me. I got them this morning from the nurse's station. I really liked them. Thank you." Most of the people who had come out of the meeting with Christian had cleared out. I double checked and then tiptoed and planted a kiss on his cheek.

"It was no big deal," Christian said modestly. "I just wanted to give you something special."

"Well it was definitely special," I said. 'Maybe I can show you *how* special a little later on."

"That sounds amazing," Christian said. He

was looking at me like he was ready to jump my bones right then and there.

"I've gotta go and start my day, but I'll text you," I said.

"I'll be looking forward to it," he replied.

Christian headed off down the hall in one way and I went the other. I checked in with Stella and got my day started. The day was busy as per usual but I powered through it. When I finally managed to get a break, I headed upstairs to Miles' room. I hadn't had a chance to go see him when I first came in.

At that point the nurses on his floor were more than used to seeing me up there. The good thing was that they were cool about it. They didn't ask me too many questions about anything and as far as I knew, they weren't gossiping about me either.

I knocked on Miles' door to let him know that I was coming in. He was sitting up in his bed doing something on his phone but put it down when he saw me.

"Good mor—" I started but my words were cut off by him.

"If there was ever a way for me to thank you," Miles began in his deep voice. His hazel eyes were focused on me intently in a way that made my body feel hot. "For all the things you've done. I'd do it over and over again, cause to me you're a special one."

I gasped. "Wait, that was you? The flowers and the poem?" I moved closer to his bed so that I was at his side.

"Yeah, who else would it be? I wanted to say thank you and I thought this was the easiest way to do it. I know I've said it a lot but I wanted to show it," Miles explained.

A moment of annoyance crossed my face. Christian's ass had let me go right on believing that he'd been the one who'd sent the flowers, but it wasn't him at all. I pushed those thoughts from my mind temporarily to focus on Miles.

"I appreciate it. I don't want you to get me gifts anymore," I said. "It's not something that we should be doing."

"But you gave me the gift of life. I can't repay you for that so I felt the need to get you something," Miles said.

Miles was smooth, I could give him that much. He knew the best ways to charm a woman and he was using all of them on me. I knew that we were getting closer and closer to blurring that line. I didn't know how he felt or anything, but I thought that maybe we should at least talk about it.

"Miles...I...look," I stammered trying to get the words out. In my head everything was fine but trying to put them into sentences wasn't working for me. "We should talk."

"Later," Miles said.

"What? Why?" I asked.

"Let's go for my afternoon walk," he said. "Unless you don't have the time."

"But I was trying to talk to you," I said.

"Let's walk and talk," he responded. He was clearly someone who was used to getting his way. Before I could say anything else, he'd already thrown the cover off of himself and was making his way to the other side of the bed where his walker was.

His t-shirt was partially raised up in the back so I could see his muscular back, which also had tattoos on it. His skin and was smooth and for the briefest of moments I wondered what it would be like to run my hand across it.

I got up and offered to help him get to his walker. I'd watched Miles struggle with this during his rehab with other people. He took offense to people helping him so I was surprised that he welcomed my help.

He said that he wanted to go back up to the roof. We made our way to one of the two elevators that took us there and headed up. We stepped out into the bright day. It was still warm but incredibly windy which was just typical of Chicago.

"It's beautiful up here. I still can't get over how nice the view is," Miles said as we walked over to one of the benches with a view of the city.

"I know. I come up here sometimes when it gets too stressful inside," I said. It almost felt romantic being there with him.

"So look, I wanted to talk to you about something," Miles said.

"What is it?"

"I should be getting out of here soon enough. I'm getting better every day. When I get out of here, I wanna take you out. Like on a date. A real one. Not just us bumping up and down these cold halls," he said with a laugh.

"Miles, that's what I wanted to talk to you about. I don't want you to think that...well I don't want to hurt your feelings or anything like that. I'm just not sure about it. You're one of my patients," I said. "It's just that it makes things complicated."

"I'm here if you change your mind, or make it up," Miles said. He didn't seem offended by my confusion in the least. I also loved that he wasn't trying to push me into making a decision the way that I knew Christian would as well.

"And you're not upset?" I asked.

"Upset?" he asked with a smirk. "A slow yes is better than a quick no." Miles stood up and extended his hand for me to grab. The two of us got up and spent the rest of the time walking and talking with one another.

When we got back to his room, Miles plopped down on the bed and checked his phone.

"I'm about to head back to my shift," I said. "By the way, what'd you say you did again?" We'd developed a running joke between us. I would ask him what he did and he'd always say the same thing.

"I'll tell you when I get out of the hospital," Miles replied with a smirk.

I turned to leave the room but bumped right into one of the guys that usually came to visit

Miles. He was bigger than me so I was moved back while he stood still. He put his hand on my arm to steady me.

"I'm sorry about that," he said. He was brown skinned and dressed in a pair of dark pants with a t-shirt and light jacket.

"No, it's my fault. I should have been looking where I was going," I said. I hurried out of the room

When I bumped into Miles' friend, his jacket had opened up some and I saw a gun tucked into his waist. It wasn't my first time seeing one, but I wondered what he did that meant he needed to carry a gun to the hospital, and why was he always seeing Miles?

CHAPTER 17

The rest of my day was pretty quiet. I was grateful for it too since Miles had given me a lot to think about. I think him asking me out made everything more real. We knew what was going on between us even if we never admitted it. However, now that the offer was on the table, it was forcing me to really think about it.

I got home that night with a mission. I sat down in the chair in front of my desk and opened my computer. I poured myself a glass of wine and got to work.

I was going to get online and look up some information on Miles. I knew that it sounded a little crazy but I wanted to know more about him, especially since he seemed to tense up whenever he talked about his current life. I had this one image of him built up in my head but he could have been someone else for real.

I knew that his real name was Miles Wilson. I decided the best places to start would be social media. His name was a common one so I narrowed down my search to people from Chicago and the surrounding area. Nothing came up, or at least nothing that could have been him. I went from one site to the next but couldn't find anything. I checked the address that he'd registered under and saw that it was someone else's.

"Hmm," I wondered out loud. Miles was young. We were in the same age bracket. The chances of him not coming up on social media were slim but they were still there. There was also the fact that he clearly had money. To be so youthful and so successful without anyone knowing what you did was rare

I wasn't about to be deterred. Google was still free, so I hopped on there and typed in "Miles Wilson." I did the same thing that I'd done on the other websites and played around with my words. I knew it might have been a long shot, but I typed in "Miles Wilson Chicago Crime." I could practically hear Stella in the back of my mind telling me that he was a criminal.

I scrolled down the page slowly, trying to see anything that popped out. I saw an article from four years ago talking about a "Miles Wilson, 21 years old." I clicked on it and read through it.

The article was short, sweet, and to the point. Miles had been charged with being the getaway driver for an armed robbery but was acquitted on all charges. I clicked through some more articles trying to find out more about what happened but that had basically been it. It was strange because usually something like that would have been mentioned a few times in the news.

I felt bad for trying to snoop into Miles' life. I knew that he'd promised that he'd tell me what he did when he got out of the hospital but I couldn't wait. After seeing that guy with the gun earlier, I just knew that there was more to him than he'd initially let on.

I sipped my wine and decided to call Stella to let her know what I'd found out. I dialed her number and she picked up after a few rings.

"Hello?" Stella answered.

"Hey Doctor, what you up to?" I asked.

"Nothing much. I've been in bed since I got home earlier. I can't figure out if I'm just tired or getting sick," she said.

"Well get some rest either way," I said. "So, I call because I've been doing some digging."

"That sounds juicy," she said with interest. "Who you looking up? You found out something about Christian?"

"No, not him," I said, "Miles."

"Oh," she said flatly. She sounded like a kid who'd just had their balloon popped. "So, what'd you find?"

"Well, I found an article. I'm pretty sure it's about him. It was from four years ago," I said.

"What happened?" she asked.

"There was some kind of armed robbery and he was the getaway driver," I explained. "Or allegedly the driver. He was brought up on charges but he got acquitted of everything."

"Doesn't surprise me," Stella said.

I knew that she didn't approve of me and Miles and whatever was or wasn't happening with us. "There was something else too," I said.

I'd been debating about whether or not to tell her, but Stella was my friend.

"What is it?" She asked me.

"Well, and I could be wrong, but I'm pretty sure that one of those guys who always comes to visit him had a gun with him today," I said.

"A gun?" Stella's voice got louder. "Are you sure? I can't believe he got that shit past security. Did anyone else see it?"

"I don't think so," I said. "I wouldn't have seen it myself if I hadn't bumped right into him."

"I'm sure it's not the first time someone brought a gun into the hospital, but I still don't like it," Stella said.

"I know what you mean." I took a long sip of my wine. "I was thinking that maybe if you could give me more information about Miles, I could find out more. You have admin privileges to the records."

"Nope," Stella replied flatly. "Not gonna happen, Kallie."

"Damn, can you at least think about it?" I pleaded. I knew that the things I'd found could only be the tip of the iceberg and I wanted to see how deep it went. The issue was that the only thing I knew about Miles were his first and last name and that he was from the Southside. I couldn't even be sure that the birthdate that he was registered under was his own.

"Kallie, I'm not interested in anything having to do with Miles and you shouldn't be either. Outside of the fact that he's a patient, he's also clearly trouble. It's written all over him. I don't know why you can't see it," Stella was clearly over the conversation. She could be really stubborn at times and I could see that this was one of them.

"Alright," I said. "I'll drop it for now. I'll let you go. I'm about to go watch some TV. I'll call you back."

"Ok, cool," Stella said.

I was actually glad to be off the phone with her. I knew that she was just trying to look out for me but she just didn't get what I was trying to do. I knew that I was playing with fire but it would be easier for me to just move on once I'd found out more about Miles. I just wanted to get some more information about who he really was.

I was about to get back to my search to see if there was anything else I could find out when the phone rang again. It was Christian calling this time around. I thought about not answering but figured it would probably be best to talk to him now than later.

"Hey Christian," I answered in a monotone.

"What's goin' on? How's your evening going?" He asked. It sounded like he was driving.

"Fine, and yours?" I was keeping it short with him.

"It's going alright," he said. "I thought I'd give you a call since you said you'd hit me up later on."

"Yeah, I'm busy tonight," I declared. I wasn't trying to start an argument but he'd definitely pulled some bullshit on me earlier.

"Really? All of a sudden you're busy? I don't know what's happening here Kallie, but I don't like it."

"You know what I don't like, Christian? People who lie about giving gifts," I countered.

"What are you talking about?"

"Don't play stupid, Christian, you're much too smart for that. If you didn't send me the flowers, why would you lie and say that you did?" I asked. I could feel my blood boiling. I was incredibly upset. "And it's not even just about the flowers. You keep claiming you wanna be with me and take things more serious but you've never done anything sweet like that before."

"Hold the fuck up," Christian spat out angrily, "you're out here getting flowers from some other dude and you got the nerve to be trying to flip this shit on me? Who you been sleeping with? There's no other reason a man would be sending you flowers."

My night only seemed to be going from bad to worse. I pulled the phone away from my ear and looked at it as though it would be able to tell me who Christian was talking to as it couldn't have been me.

"Are you fucking serious?" I almost yelled into the phone. "If I was sleeping with someone else, I would tell you about it, unlike you. I still didn't forget all that shit with Ashley from before. Not to mention the fact that if I *was* sleeping with someone else, they'd have sent me a lot more than some flowers and a note."

Christian sounded like a hurt child when he spoke again. "My...my bad, Kallie. I just wanted to try and explain—"

"No, you've done enough explaining for one night," I said. "Actually, you know what, Christian? I think that whatever this is between us has run its course. I'm done."

"Run its course? What does that mean?" he asked.

"You heard me. I'm done. We're done. I don't like where this is going and haven't for a while," I explained.

The smug Christian was back again. "Not the first time I've heard this before. You'll be back before long," he said. I opened my mouth to speak but he hung up the phone before I could get another word out.

I ended up finishing the rest of that bottle of wine that night. I couldn't believe that everyone was trying me the way that they were. Stella had almost chewed my head off and then Christian started up with his mess. I was glad that I'd finally made the decision to end things with him for real. He was definitely starting to become more trouble than he was worth.

Over the course of the next few days, I focused on work. There was always something to do; a patient to see or a prescription to write.

It was easy to get caught up in that instead of sitting around being upset with Christian.

Miles and I seemed to be doing alright. I was worried that our conversation from before and my uneasiness about going out with him might have affected things with us but he acted like it hadn't happened. I watched over those next few days as he worked hard to make himself better and finally it was time for him to be released from the hospital.

Miles had been a patient for almost a month. It might not seem like a long time to some but to become used to seeing someone every day and then to not have them around would definitely be a change for me. I was going to miss him, even if I didn't want to admit it.

Miles asked me to walk him downstairs. I was glad to be spending those last few moments in the hospital with him. He had moved on from using the walker and had graduated to a cane. He needed it more for balance than anything but I suspected that after a week or so he'd be back to his normal self.

Stepping out into the bright light of the morning sun with Miles felt different. I assumed it was because it meant that he was officially no long a patient of mine. It could also have been the fact that for the first time, I finally got a chance to see what he looked like as a regular person and not in sweats, shorts, or a hospital robe.

Miles was wearing a gray and black designer t-shirt. Around his neck was a thin gold chain with a gold cross and diamonds at the end of it. His jeans looked expensive and if his sneakers weren't fresh out of the box, I would have been surprised.

"How are you getting home?" I asked.

Almost on cue, a black SUV pulled up in front of us in the drive of the hospital. In the front seat I could see one of the guys who'd constantly visited Miles. We walked around to the passenger side of the door and he opened it and turned to me.

"I told myself that I would just wait on you, but I can't," he said. "Just go out with me. One time. Nothing crazy, just dinner or something like that."

"I would like that but it's just not a good time," I explained. "I'm kind of going through a breakup or something like that. It's just complicated."

"Aight, not a problem," he said as he climbed into the front of the car.

"So, you're out now," I said with a sad smirk. "Aren't you gonna tell me what it is that you do?"

I felt like I was getting my answer right there. The dude who was sitting next to Miles pressed some button and a little compartment opened up on the dashboard. Miles reached into it and grabbed a gun, shoving it into his waist. He tried to move quickly to cover it up but it was too late. I'd seen it.

I took a step back from him and he hopped out of the car. He walked closer to me but dropped his head as if he was in shame. He was tall as hell but looked like a sad little boy.

"I'm not like you, at least not in a lot of ways," Miles said when he finally lifted his head. "I know we grew up under similar circumstances and stuff but you know how everybody has their own path to take? Mine ain't take me to medical school, it took me to the streets."

"How...how'd you—"

"Get shot?" He completed the sentence and I nodded my head. "It was some dumb shit. It was a deal that went wrong. I'm usually not on the scene too often so when I showed up at a spot, somebody decided that they wanted to try and take me out. It wasn't pretty, but I made it. I won't get caught slipping like that ever again."

"Miles, I..." My voice trailed off as I tried to think of something to say.

He just shook his head. "Nah, it's cool. I can already see that it's a little different now," he said sadly. "You even look a little scared of me now."

I shook my head. "I'm not scared. I'm just...this is a lot for me to take in."

"I know," he said. "And I'm not trying to have you take it all in right now. I wanted to tell you in my own way and at my own time. I just don't want you to look at me differently because of this. I just wanted to say thank you again. Not just for saving my life, but for this little break. It was nice to be here with you. You talked a lot about being legit and for a minute there I thought that I could be one of those suit and tie, 9 to 5 kind of dudes...like you deserve."

I couldn't think of anything to say. On top of everything that had happened the night before, I now had a new batch of information that I needed to process.

Miles leaned in and kissed me on the cheek. "I'll see you around, Kallie. You got my number if you need anything," he said.

Miles climbed back into the truck and they pulled off leaving me confused.

CHAPTER 18

I headed back into the hospital after Miles left. I went through the rest of the day in somewhat of a daze. I was trying to process everything that he'd told me. It was a lot to take in. Miles had been a mystery to me for a long time. We'd been connecting with one another throughout the entire time that he'd been in the hospital and I'd been waiting for him to tell me more about himself. Now that he had, I only seemed to have more questions.

My day seemed to drag after he left. Miles had been discharged in the morning so I had the entire day to go through without him. I tried to cheer myself up, but I was just in a mood. I had so much on my mind that when I got home that night I couldn't even really sleep. I tossed and turned trying to calm my thoughts but it wouldn't work. I was glad that I had the following day off.

When I got up the following day I headed to the gym. It was the only thing that I could think of to take my mind off of Miles. After I headed home later that day and realized that I had a full day ahead of me and no plans, I decided to make some.

I tried to convince myself that I was calling Miles to end my boredom but it was really just because I missed him. I hadn't realized until he was gone how much I really had grown to care about him. I dialed his number and he answered after two rings.

"What's up Kallie?" His deep voice answered the phone. There was music playing in his background but it sounded like he walked away from it. I loved how he'd answered the phone as if he was waiting for me to call.

"Hey. How are you?" I answered.

"Good, and you?"

"I'm alright, just chillin on my day off," I said. I wasn't really too good at small talk. I always found myself repeating the same things.

"So, is your offer still on the table? You know, the one about taking me out? I mean, you are out of the hospital now."

"Yeah, we can do that. I'd like that," he replied.

I couldn't help but smile. "What time is good for you?" I asked.

"How about I send someone to pick you up around seven tonight?" Miles said.

"Seven?" I asked. It was a little early, but I assumed he might have had some other plans or something.

"Yeah. I got a place in mind that we could go but it's a little drive away," he explained. "It's a nice restaurant so wear something nice, not that that's ever been an issue for you."

"Alright, so seven it is," I said. "I'll see you then."

"Cool. I'll see you," he said before he hung up the phone.

The same butterflies that I'd been feeling when I was around Miles were coming back to me even stronger now. I felt like I was buzzing with energy for the rest of the day. I took a nap and then got up to start getting ready.

It would be my first time going out with

Miles and I couldn't believe how nervous I was. I felt like nothing in my closet was nice enough. Finally, I settled on something that was sexy but didn't do too much. I put on a red cocktail dress that complimented my butter pecan skin. It showed off my legs and cleavage while also hugging my curves. I decided to leave my hair down and sprayed some stuff in it to make it even curlier. I put on a pair of heels and checked myself out in the mirror.

"You look good, girl," I said to my reflection as I did a little dance in the mirror.

My phone started to ring. It was Miles letting me know that my ride was downstairs. I grabbed my purse and headed downstairs. My doorman, Tony, couldn't help but to compliment me as I walked out of the building.

There was a black BMW sitting at the curb right outside. I wasn't sure if that was it or not until the back door opened and Miles stepped out of it. I'd seen him in regular clothes before but seeing him as dressed up as he was just confirmed to me that I was making the right choice. No one who looked that good could have been bad for me.

Miles was dressed in a pair of black dress

pants that hugged his muscular legs. He was wearing a white button-down shirt with the top two buttons open, showing off his tattoos, particularly the one on his neck that was the most interesting. His dark brown, wavy hair was perfectly groomed and when I got up to him, I could smell one of the expensive colognes that he'd kept at his bedside when he was a patient. One woman who was walking passed was trying to do her best not to stare but Miles looked like he'd just stepped out of a magazine, so it was hard not to.

I noticed there was a guy sitting in the front of the car in the driver's seat but he hadn't gotten out. I walked up to Miles and he wrapped his arms around me before planting a kiss firmly on my cheek.

"You look good," he said to me.

"Thanks," I said. "So do you."

"I try," he smirked. "You ready?"

I nodded my head. "Yeah, let's go."

The two of us got into the car. It was nice on the inside as well. I was pretty sure that it was the updated version of the car that Christian drove which was ironic in itself.

"I think you remember my boy, Keith," he

said indicating the guy sitting in the front. As he pulled off he waved his hand at me.

"Nice to see you again," I said. I hadn't really spoken to any of the guys when they visited Miles in the hospital but it was nice to have a name to put to a face.

I turned my attention back to Miles. "Where's your cane?" I asked.

He playfully rolled his eyes. "Oh God," he said with a smile on his face, "we're not doing this tonight."

"Doing what?"

"This whole doctor thing," he said. "I know it's in you to worry, but just relax. I'm not using that cane unless I have to. Besides, it doesn't go with my outfit."

I couldn't help but to laugh at his joke. "Fine, I'll leave all the medical stuff at home tonight," I responded. "Dr. Jameson is at home. You just have Kallie tonight."

"That's all I need," Miles said flirtatiously.

"So, where's this place that we're going to?" I asked out of curiosity.

"It's this spot that I heard about a while ago. I heard the food was really good but I never found anyone to go there with...until now of course," he explained. "It's far. Like, we'd be leaving the city far. Nothing too crazy though. Don't want you to think I'm trying to kidnap you."

I laughed again. "I trust you," I said. "But what makes you wanna go to a place so far away? Chicago has some of the best restaurants in the whole state."

Miles sighed. "Honestly, I need to lay low. I'm not trying to go to places that I normally go to cause some people might be looking for me. I wasn't planning on coming back out for a while but I couldn't resist it when you called me."

I was a little taken aback by him saying that people were looking for him. Miles and I were a part of two different worlds and this was just a taste of his.

"Are you sure it's...safe?" I asked.

Miles nodded his head. "You're always safe with me. I can take care of you."

"I'm from the Southside, same as you. I can handle myself," I said with a little smirk.

"I bet," Miles responded.

The two of us enjoyed one another's company as we headed to the restaurant. When we finally arrived, he told his guy to go park and he'd let him know when to pull back up.

"This is nice," I said. We were on the side of a hotel at the entrance for its restaurant. We stepped inside and were greeted by a hostess. Miles told them his name and we got a table.

"You made reservations?" I asked as we sat down. We were seated in the back of the restaurant in a corner.

"Yeah. Once you said yes I figured it would just be easier. This place fills up quickly. I heard rappers come and eat here when they're in town," he explained.

"You have good taste," I replied.

"In restaurants and in women," Miles flirted back. I couldn't help but to blush.

The waitress came over to us and gave us water and menus. Miles asked if I was thirsty and ended up ordering us a bottle of wine. The waitress brought it over to us and placed it on the table.

"This is delicious," I said, taking a sip of the freshly poured wine.

"Yeah, it is good," Miles responded. His low hazel eyes focused on mine. "So, what did you do all day since you were off?"

I took another sip of the wine. "Worked out. Ran some errands. Nothing too much. I'm a workaholic so on my days off I try to relax but it's kind of hard to."

"Yeah, I know how that can be," Miles said. "Always on the go. Always moving around. It takes reminders sometimes to just stop and take a deep breath."

"Exactly," I agreed. He hadn't directly mentioned it but since he was hinting at work I decided to press him for more information. "So how are things with your...work? I have to admit that I was definitely surprised yesterday when you told me what you told me."

This time Miles didn't look down but his jaw clenched tighter. "You were surprised?" He asked.

I nodded my head. "Yeah. I think that after getting to know you for so long that I'd just kind of built up this image of you in my head."

"You're something else," Miles said with a smile.

"Why's that?" I asked.

"You think I don't know what everybody thought about me in the hospital?" He asked. He raised his hands up a little bit. "This is

Chicago. Someone like me coming into an emergency room looking the way that I did probably only meant one thing to most people. But, not to you. That's some real shit."

I blushed again. "I try not to judge people by their looks," I said. What he was saying was true though. I might have heard it from Stella often but there were definitely other whispers around the hospital about Miles and most of them weren't good.

"It's probably cause you're from the same place as me," he said.

"Yeah, but I'm far removed from a lot of that stuff," I replied. "I haven't been to the Southside in a long time. I don't have a reason to go over there really."

"Yeah, I wish I didn't have to," he said in a dark way. "But enough about all that other stuff. What's going on with you?"

Miles and I sat at the table and talked for the next two hours. I realized that he just wouldn't talk about his work with me until we got closer and I was actually fine with that. I hated to admit it, but for as much as I liked him, I was still uncomfortable sometimes. I think a lot of it had to do with the fact that he said that whoever had shot him was still looking for him. I wasn't dumb. All this cloak and dagger stuff that he tried to play off at romance was also for safety. I knew he had to be strapped and so was his boy.

His friend, associate, or whatever he was, came back after we finished up and drove us back to my spot. When we got there, Miles asked if he could take me to my door. I was a little apprehensive but when he said that he wasn't trying to come inside I decided to let him.

"Did you enjoy yourself?" I asked Miles as we stepped off the elevator and made our way down the hall to my apartment.

"I did," he said. "What about you?"

I nodded my head. "I had a great time."

"So, before you go inside I just wanted to say something," Miles and I had just gotten to my apartment door.

"What's up?"

"I know you're still trying to figure all of this out. I can see it on your face," he said. When I tried to say something, Miles just put a finger on my lips. "Nah, it's cool. I'm not even about to trip. I know all of this might be a lot for you, but, I just wanted to let you know for sure that

I'm serious about this. I like you and I wanna get to know you. You help me get my mind off of things."

"I think I'd like that," I said. I unlocked the door to my apartment and held it open for just a second or two longer, thinking about risking it all and inviting Miles inside. I decided against it. I did however turn around and grab Miles by the back of the head and placed my lips firmly on his. Our first kiss was nothing short of amazing. His full, brown sugar colored lips were soft as we kissed. I was so close to inviting him inside but instead I broke the kiss and told him good night.

That first date with Miles turned out the be just the beginning. What was happening with us came from nowhere but was growing into something that was becoming a big part of both of our lives.

The two of us started going out with one another all the time. We usually ended up leaving the city or being far from my neighborhood, but it was fine because Miles always had something planned. Whether it was different types of restaurants or activities, he always had it covered.

The best part of it all was how much we talked. He told me more and more about himself. Though he still hadn't gotten too much into what went on with work, I didn't mind after a while. There was so much more to him than most people would have guessed. He was a deep thinker and an amazing listener. The two of us would talk about our dreams and our goals with one another. We'd sit down and have real conversations about how to get the things that we wanted out of life. If it was important to me, it was important to him and vice versa.

We got to the point where we had to be real with ourselves and admit that what was happening between us was more than just a friendship. Our attraction was undeniable. We hadn't talked about labels or anything with us, but it wasn't even necessary. We knew what it was.

One day I'd gotten out of work in the middle of the day after an early morning shift. I'd texted Miles earlier in the day and invited him over for dinner. He was a little surprised since we always went out but he was with it. He asked me if I wanted him to get me some dinner but I told him that I'd be cooking dinner that night.

At around seven that evening there was a knock on the door. I had literally just finished taking the food out of the oven when he arrived so it was right on time.

I still had my apron on but smoothed it down as I made my way to the door, flinging it open. Miles was standing there looking as well put together as he always did. His cologne wafted in the house as he walked in. He greeted me with a peck on the cheek. Miles and I had been affectionate with one another but still hadn't had sex or even gone too far in that direction. It was refreshing to me because we had lots of time to really get to know one another.

"Damn, it smells good in here," Miles said. He took in a big, deep breath. "What's that?" His eyes got wide as he looked around trying to find the source of the smell.

"I told you I was cooking," I said with a pleased smile on my face. He hadn't even tasted anything and I could practically see the drool on his lips.

"Yeah, you said cooking, not five-star chefing it up," he joked.

"I hope you're hungry," I said as I grabbed him by the hand and led him to the dining area by the window. I liked looking out at the city while I ate.

"Starving," he replied. "What'd you make?"

"I made us some rib eye steaks with potatoes and asparagus," I said.

I told Miles to go and wash his hands. When he came back I'd already laid the food out on the table. Two huge steaks, cooked to perfection, sat on the table.

"Yo, this shit looks good," Miles said as he sat back down. He couldn't help but to take another long whiff of the food.

"And it tastes good too," I said. "I found a good butcher and got some imported beef."

"You didn't have to do all that for me," he said. I could tell he was appreciative of it all.

"I didn't. I've got two more steaks in the freezer for whenever I want them," I said with a smirk.

"You're real fancy," Miles smiled.

Miles and I enjoyed our dinner. From the first bite he couldn't stop talking to me about how much he loved it. He kept asking me if I'd taken cooking classes or anything because the steak was so tender.

After dinner, the two of us had the "itis." We sluggishly moved over to the couch and plopped down. A show that we both wanted to watch was on, so we ended up cuddling on the big couch and watching it. Miles was laying behind me with one of his arms loosely draped over me. He kept asking me if I was comfortable but after a few minutes all I could hear were the sounds of him sleeping. It wasn't long until I drifted off as well.

Buzz.

Buzz.

Buzz.

The sounds of the vibrations on the table woke both of us up. After all the steak and wine Miles and I had collapsed on the couch but the sounds of his phone had woken us up. When we'd first laid down there had still been a little bit of sunlight left but by the time we woke up there was nothing in the sky but city lights and stars.

Miles started to move and then me. His arm was still wrapped around me and I'd snuggled closer to him in my sleep. My phone was still on the kitchen table but Miles had brought his over to the living room and put it on the table.

"Fuck," Miles said. His voice was extra deep since he'd just woken up.

"What is it?" I asked.

"This fuckin' phone. Shit kept waking me up," he said with a yawn. "Damn, I ain't mean to fall asleep."

"We were both tired and full off the food," I replied. Miles tried to stretch his hand out over me to grab his phone but I grabbed his arm and pulled it down.

"What you doing?"

"If they're calling or texting now, they'll keep doing it. Just relax. You always talk about how you never have enough time to just relax, right?" I was enjoying being laid up with him.

"You right," he said. "I shouldn't have stayed knowing I got stuff to do but I just felt so good laying here with you." Miles dropped his arm and pulled himself closer to me, burying his face in my neck.

I was feeling caught up in being with Miles. He was working out to be everything that I wanted in someone. He paid attention to me.

He talked to me like I was his equal and most importantly, I was comfortable with him. When I was around Miles I didn't feel as though I needed to do anything extra. I felt as though I could completely be myself and it wouldn't be a problem at all. Laying on the couch with him, not really doing anything but enjoying him, reminded me of that.

"What time is it?" Miles asked.

"I'm not sure. Probably late but I don't think we were sleeping for too long," I answered.

"I can stay till the morning if you want. We don't have to do nothing'. We can just kick it on the couch," Miles said. I was glad that he wasn't in a rush to head out either.

"I'd like that," I replied. "But, let me get up and use the bathroom."

"Alright."

When I came back from the bathroom Miles was sitting up on the couch. His phone was in his hands, but he put it back down when I walked into the room. I sat on the couch, resting my back against the arm of it and putting my legs across his lap.

Miles' hands started to rub my legs on top

of my jeans. "I got something to tell you," he said.

"What is it?" I sat up with urgency. He'd just been looking at his phone so there were a number of things he could have been talking about."

"Chill," he said. "Nothing serious. Well it's serious stuff but nothing to be worried about."

"I'm all ears," I said. "You know you can talk to me about anything."

Miles looked up at me with a serious look on his face. "I ever told you how I got into the game?"

I shook my head. My heartbeat sped up a little bit. "No."

Miles was still rubbing my leg but his head turned away from me. It was like he was having a flashback.

"When I was a youngin', I knew this dude around the way. If I was 13, he had to be at least 10 years older," he began. "Dude's name was Big Jimmy. He was this fat dude. Like, real fat. Obese kind of fat. The funny thing about him was that for as fat as he was, you never really saw him without a bad bitch on his side.

"Anyway, Big Jimmy had a crew of dudes

with him. He was big time in the hood. He wasn't an OG yet only cause of age but even the OG's respected him. Jimmy saw me one day after I'd just gotten into a fight. Some niggas tried to jump me. I ain't win but I ain't lose either. Either way, Jimmy saw something in me that day and he wanted me to come work for him."

"And you did it?' I asked. He'd only been speaking for a minute but I was hanging onto his every word like it was a good book.

Miles shook his head. "Nah, not at all. I don't take orders well and from the way that Jimmy described it, I'd be a fuckin' corner boy forever. I wasn't with it at all."

"So what'd you do?"

"I got my own crew and got them working for me," he explained. "It was just me and few of my own people. Most of them still work with me today. We took over a couple of corners or whatever. Jimmy noticed. He approached me again but this time he came correct." Miles turned his head to me and looked me in the eye. "People wanna act like there are no rules on the street but that's a lie. Jimmy knew that everything I was doing was to impress him and when he stepped to me this time around, it wasn't to get a corner or two. He wanted me in his crew in an upper position."

Miles got quiet after that. "And what ended up happening to Jimmy?"

"The streets don't love nobody," he replied. "Same shit that happened to Jimmy is the same thing people are trying to do to me. Niggas get jealous and want everything that you have. The difference between Jimmy and I is ain't nobody taking me out."

"Is that what's going on with you now?" I asked. "Is that why we always have to go out of the city for dates and stuff?"

Miles nodded his head. "In this game people get greedy. Niggas want what doesn't belong to them. With Jimmy it was a robbery gone wrong. With me, they're trying to take my territory. I'm at war right now for some space that people want. That's why I don't talk too much about what's going on with me. I don't wanna stress you out about it."

"I can't be protected from everything," I said to him.

"Yeah, I know," he said in a way that sounded bitter. "This war that I'm in has gotten out of hand. These new dudes coming up don't have respect. It was them that hurt me. They almost took me out. Now I'm in a position to make hard decisions and I don't want to, even though I know I need to."

I took my legs off of him and shifted my body around so I could lay my head on his lap. Miles started to run his fingers through my hair. "So the other gang made it worse?"

"Mmm-hmm," he said with a nod. "It's getting blown out of proportion. People are dying."

"Have you...?" My voice trailed off in the question but Miles knew where my mind was headed.

"I don't like hurting people," he said cryptically. "But sometimes things come with the territory that you can't avoid. I just want peace. Everybody can get money, but I don't think it's close to being done."

"What made you wanna talk about all of this all of a sudden?"

"Honestly, I feel like you need to know," Miles said. "I don't want you to be afraid of anything, but I do want you to be informed. One of my lieutenants' girl almost got snatched up. When they couldn't take her, they almost killed her, but she ran." Miles put his other hand on my waist. "I don't want you to worry about none of that. As far as I know, no one but my people know we're together so you should be safe. I'm just scared that if someone finds out what you are to me that they'll come after you."

"Is that a possibility?" I asked. I wasn't afraid but I did need to know.

Miles shook his head. "Not as long as I'm around," he said.

CHAPTER 19

C alling my day long would have been an understatement. It had been hell. An old man had come in after his wife came home and found him passed out on the floor. He'd had a heart attack. We tried to do as much for him as we could but we ended up losing him. I knew that it was just a part of the job but I always felt bad about it. I always made sure to pray for any of the people I lost.

I was exhausted as I stepped out of the hospital. I'd gotten to work a little late so I wasn't able to park in the hospital's parking garage. There was a big parking lot outside the back that a lot of people used. I wasn't too fond of it though because it was too dark and security was only at the front.

I looked around, not seeing anyone else in the lot. My car was parked in a middle row on the left-hand side, close to a gate. I pulled my keys from my bag as I got closer and unlocked the door. Opening the backseat, I threw my purse into it and closed it.

I had just opened the driver's door and was about to climb inside when I felt a big hand grab my arm. I was pushed forward, slamming the door in front of me. My whole body was pushed up against the car as I struggled to try and get free. My arm was being held and twisted against my back, making it harder for me to move. I was trying to kick up with my legs but I kept on missing.

Whoever was holding me started to grab at my clothes. Terror went through my body like electricity. My eyes got wide and I started to try and struggle more.

I opened my mouth and let out a scream. I was about to let out another when I heard the clicking of a gun and felt the metal of its barrel press against my head.

"Scream again and see if I don't kill you

bitch," a deep raspy voice said. I closed my mouth and held it tight. I was afraid. I just prayed that I would make it out of this situation alive.

When I didn't say anything else the guy kept on talking. "Damn, you must have some good pussy if it got Miles out here slippin' up like this. I'm gonna get me some before I blow your ass up."

There were more sounds behind me. First there was the jingling of a belt. No more than a second after that I heard a loud thud that and then a groan. The hands that were holding onto me let me go and I heard another loud sound as someone dropped to the floor.

I quickly turned around to see what had happened. There was one man dressed all in black on the floor. It was dark but I could see a small pool of blood forming from underneath him. Two men were standing over him. One of them I didn't know but the other I recognized as Keith, Miles' friend.

Everything started to happen so fast. A car pulled up next to mine. It was a simple navy blue four door, something very nondescript. The driver of that car got out and opened the door while the two guys who were standing by me lifted the man who'd been stabbed and put him into the back.

"Just relax. Miles figured something like this might happen," Keith said. I was still stuck on stupid after all that had taken place over the course of the last three minutes.

One of the guys who'd been helping to put the other guy into the back came over to my car. The keys were still in the door. He didn't ask as he got in and looked around. He looked in the backseat and even popped the trunk. I wasn't sure what he was looking for but once he was satisfied that he *hadn't* found it, he climbed in the driver's seat.

I thought he was going to drive me home, so I made a move to head towards the passenger's seat. Instead I was steered towards another car.

"You can't take your car. Someone might be looking for it. Miles will explain more," Keith said. My head was still in a fog, so I just weakly nodded my head and went along with it.

I drove home with who I assumed was another one of Miles' friends or workers. He explained to me that he was taking a longer way to my house in case someone was following us. I couldn't believe all of what happened and even now that it was continuing it felt like someone else's life and not mine.

When we finally pulled up outside of my building, Miles was already in front. He was pacing and walking back and forth but he hung up with whoever he was talking to when he saw the car. He walked up to my door and pulled it open.

Thankfully I'd recovered a little bit by then, but Miles still helped me out of the truck.

"Are you alright?" he asked. He had his hands on my shoulders and was looking at me the way that a parent looked at a child after they fell. "You good? Did that nigga hurt you? Wait till I get my hands on him!" His chest was heaving up and down. His eyes were on fire. I'd never seen him so angry before.

"I'm fine," I said. "He...didn't."

"Yo, I don't know what I'd do if something happened to you," Miles pulled me into a hug. He held me tight before breaking it. "It's too hot right now on the streets. I'm worried about you."

"Let's just go upstairs," I said. We were still standing outside of the car. I was feeling shaken up so I just wanted to be in the comfort of my own home. Miles nodded his head and the two of us went inside and up to my apartment.

Once we got inside and locked the door, I told Miles that I wanted to lay down. We headed into my bedroom and relaxed on top of the covers. He laid on his back and I rested my head on his chest.

For a long time neither of us said anything. Miles was rubbing my arm with his hand and I was just laying there thinking and breathing. If Miles hadn't of sent those guys to look out for me, who knew what could have happened? I was just thankful that it was over but my mind started to wonder about what might be coming next.

"I'm sorry I brought you into all this mess," Miles said after a while. He sounded like he'd calmed down some. He was so upset outside.

I didn't know what to say so I stayed silent.

"I'd get it if you just wanted to leave me alone. This a lot for something to handle," Miles said. I remained silent, so he went on. "Do you care about me?"

I kept the silence up but I moved my body so

I could put my head on his arm and look at him. I slowly nodded my head at him.

"I care about you too," he said. It was his turn to get quiet but it was only for a minute. "Do you have any vacation time? I think we could use a couple of days out of the city."

CHAPTER 20

Miles ended up staying with me that night. I knew that he probably had other places he could have been, but I think that him seeing me so shaken up had taken its toll on him and he wanted to make sure that I was good. I was appreciative of it because I didn't want to be alone.

When I got up the next morning I checked to see how much vacation time I had. Since I was *always* at work, I was glad to see that I'd accumulated well over three weeks' worth. I told Miles about it in the morning and told him that the earliest I'd be able to get that much time off with such short notice was the following week. He said that he wished we could go sooner but he agreed and said that he'd book everything.

I mostly went to work and minded my business that week. I was still a little shaken up but Miles made it clear to me that I was safe whether I could see it or not. I knew that he had people on me but it was fine because I didn't really go anywhere besides work, the gym, and the grocery store.

The following week arrived and Miles showed up outside of my apartment in his car. I'd asked him earlier in the week where we were going and he said that he knew it would be best for us to just get the hell out of the city so he'd booked us a hotel suite in Miami. I hadn't been to Miami in years so I was definitely excited about it.

He parked his car at the airport and we boarded a plane headed for Florida. As the plane took off, I looked out the window and watched the city get smaller and smaller. I felt all of the stress and anxiety that I'd been walking around with for a while melt off of me. It was then that I knew that this vacation was exactly what I needed to put my mind at ease.

When we landed in Miami there was a

shuttle that took us to our hotel. Miles checked in and we headed upstairs. I was amazed by the room when we got inside.

The ceiling was super high. The walls were cement gray some with kind of white design on them. There was art on the wall and all of the furniture was modern. The living room area felt like my apartment with its balcony, big couch and huge TV on the wall. The bedroom was equally as nice with a King-sized bed and huge TV. There was even a jacuzzi in the bathroom in addition to the shower.

"You sure do know how to book hotel rooms," I said to Miles as I put my bag down on the floor in the bedroom.

"Yeah, this shit is nice, right?" He replied. "It looked good on the computer but it looks better in person."

"Have you been to Miami before?" I asked.

"A few times," he said. "Mostly for business, never for pleasure."

"Well, no business this time around," I said with a smirk.

Miles put his suitcase down on the other side of the room. "Nah, nothing but pleasure this time around," he responded.

I plopped down on the bed and he climbed into it too. He was tall but the bed was way bigger than him and I felt like a child on it. "So what'd you want to do? We got here early so we have the whole day ahead of us."

"Honestly, I could take a nap," Miles said with a laugh.

"Me too!" I was glad that he'd said it. We left early in the morning and it was only early afternoon when we got off the plane.

"Alright so how about we sleep and then go out later? Like dinner or something. Maybe we could take a walk on the beach," he suggested.

"That sounds good to me," I said. I got up and headed towards the edge of the bed.

"Where you going?" Miles asked. He was already making himself comfortable, kicking his shoes of and grabbing a pillow.

"I just need to check my email real quick before I—"

I didn't get a chance to finish my sentence. Miles' long arm stretched itself out and he wrapped it around my waist. Using no strength at all, he pulled me back to him.

"No work," he said as he buried his head in my neck. "Ain't that what you just told me?"

I started to laugh. His breath all on my neck was tickling me. "Alright, alright," I said as I tried to get free. We'd only been in Miami for a little while, but I could already see the effect that it was having on Miles. He seemed to also let his guard drop.

His head was still snuggled up to my neck. What had just been breathing at first was now turning into gentle kisses. I stopped struggling and put my hand on his face as he started to kiss my neck with more passion.

I had honestly been wondering when this was going to happen. Miles and I had been chilling with one another for a while now. We'd gone out on dates, talked, and he'd ended up falling asleep at my house way more than once. We hadn't had sex though. I think at first he was waiting for me to be more comfortable and then I think he figured the time wasn't right. I was hesitant at first but once he said we'd be going on vacation with one another I knew it was only a matter of time.

Miles' firm hands rubbed on my thighs from behind me as I turned my neck to kiss him on the lips. I flipped my body so that I was facing him. His hands gripped at my ass now, squeezing it and paling it in his hand.

The gray sweatpants that he'd worn on the flight were easy access. While still kissing him, I ran my hand along the knot he'd tied and undid it. I reached my hand into his shorts and was surprised. I knew he was packing but his dick wasn't even all the way hard and it was filling up my hands. I jerked it a little bit before Miles broke the kiss to stand up.

Handsome as the day is long, Miles seemed to take his clothes off in slow motion. First his t-shirt came off exposing his white wife beater. That came off next. Miles' tattoos seemed to come alive in the sunlight shining in through the window. He dropped his pants and stood in front of me wearing a pair of gray boxes briefs. The bulge in the front looked like it might rip through the material.

Miles put his hand into his drawers and repositioned his dick. I moved to the edge of the bed and was about to take my clothes off when Miles lowered himself on top of me. I wrapped my legs around his waist and pulled my shirt off, exposing the black lace bra that I'd worn.

Miles buried himself in my breasts. He took

his time, taking one in his hand to lick and suck before he moved on to the other. Back and forth he went from one to the next. He knew what he was doing because after a while he managed to undo my jeans with one hand and helped me slip out of them.

Now that my panties were off Miles was taking time to rub and massage my thighs. I was laying on my back and he was moving his hands up and down my body. Starting at my shoulder blades, he massaged me from head to toe. He worked his hands back up and stopped them at my thigh area. He started rubbing on my ass and thighs and then slowly began to push his fingers inside of me, one at a time, and slowly.

"Ooh," I moaned as his finger went all the way inside of me. It felt good and it had been a while since I'd gotten any. Miles was about to change all of that though.

He pulled my body up so that I was in the doggy style position. He laid on his back and moved himself so that he was underneath me. I lowered my body onto his face and Miles went to work.

I sat there while that man turned me every which way but loose. He knew how to use his tongue like a weapon and I was the victim. My juices dropped on his face as he licked and sucked at me.

"Oh my God, Miles!" I moaned loudly. I was glad that the bedroom was far from the main door because I was loud. I couldn't help it. My body shook as I came. I tensed up, not trying to move. I was trying to just enjoy the intensity of it. When Miles started to lick and suck again, I knew it was time to move. I climbed off him and made my way down to his underwear.

I almost felt hungry as I pulled them off of him and threw them across the room. There was nothing but sexual chemistry between us at that point. I wanted to do to him what he'd just done to me.

Miles' dick was hard as a rock. I jerked it a little bit up and down before I put my mouth on it. Bobbing head up and down, I went to work on his dick. I had been waiting for weeks for us to finally be intimate with one another and I felt like I had something to prove. He needed to know that taking all of this time to wait for sex was worth it.

My head game was on point as I worked

him in and out of my mouth. I liked giving head because of the power I held when I did it.

"Damn baby," Miles moaned. "Ahh shit."

I kept going. I could feel his body starting to tense up. He put his hand on the back of my head and pushed my head down further.

"Fuck!" he moaned. I knew he was on the verge of coming, which was why he'd pulled my head away from him. Miles was like most men in that way; he liked head, but nothing would be better than having sex.

I didn't notice when he pulled out a couple of condoms, but they were right there on the bed. He picked up one of the gold wrappers and ripped it open with his teeth. He slid the tight fitting thing onto his dick all the way to the shaft.

"Come here," Miles said seductively. He didn't have to tell me twice as I crawled up to him. The two of us started kissing again, this time more slowly and gently. He was careful as he turned me over onto my back and positioned himself between my legs.

His dick was big so he took his time and slowly pushed it inside of me. I gasped as he went in further and further. We never broke our kiss until he was all the way inside. He held his body there for a few seconds and then started to slowly stroke me.

There was a mirror on the wall in the room and while I couldn't see my whole body because it was too high but I could see Miles. Watching his hips as he started speeding up and seeing the muscles move all over his body was turning me on.

I focused my attention on him as our eyes met. "Mmm Miles, that feels good," I moaned.

If there was anything you could do to make a man feel better, it was tell them that their sex was good. I laid there moaning and telling Miles to keep on going and he did. Finally, the two of us exploded at almost the same time. Our bodies had developed a thin layer of sweat. He collapsed on top of me breathing hard. He managed to get the condom off and pull a sheet off the two of us before we drifted off to sleep satisfied.

I don't know how long we slept for but when I got up Miles was already out of the bed. The sun had gone down. I didn't know where my clothes had been thrown to earlier in the day but Miles' shirt was on the bed with me somehow, so I put it on. When I headed into the living room, Miles was sitting on the couch half dressed. He was wearing a pair of jeans and some socks with no shirt.

"Well damn. I ain't think you were getting up anytime soon," Miles said with a smirk. "I have that effect on people."

"Oh hush," I said as I walked over to the couch and sat down next to him. "You smell good."

"Thanks. I just got out of the shower," he said. "I wanted to be ready for whenever you woke up."

I stretched my arms out and yawned. "What time is it?"

"Almost nine," he said.

"Damn, are we still gonna be able to find somewhere to eat?" I asked. "It's kind of late."

"Please, this is Miami. Places don't even get really packed till later. We can find someplace to go. You know what you want to eat?" He asked.

"I could go for some Cuban food," I answered. "We're in Miami after all."

"I'm wit' it," he said.

It took me a little over a half hour to get ready. I was in Miami so I planned on being as natural as possible. It was my vacation so I didn't feel the need to go through all the trouble of trying to straighten my hair or put on a lot of makeup.

I put on a black jumpsuit and a pair of heels. The jumpsuit showed off a lot of skin on top but was still super classy. My curly hair flowed freely down my back and I put on a pair of big earrings to finish it off. Miles had put on a white button-down shirt and changed his sneakers to a pair of shoes. The two of us looked so good together that I had to snap a picture.

Miles and I headed to a place that he'd looked up online. We took a cab there and it was nice to see the city as we drove over the water. I was having a great time already.

"This food is delicious," I said. We were seated at a small Cuban place. It was a little more upscale than some of the other places, but I could tell why. The food was amazing.

"It melts in your mouth it's so good," Miles commented. "I'm glad we came here."

"Me too," I said. "And not just this restaurant. I'm glad that we had this chance to get away from Chicago and forget about everything that's been going on."

"So am I," he agreed. "I've been thinking about something and I wanna know how you feel about it."

"What's on your mind?" I asked.

"So, we've been chillin', dating, whatever you wanna call it for a while now. I wanna make it official," he said. "I know from before that you had your reservations but I feel like we're in a better place now."

I smiled brightly. Miles knew how to express himself in a way that was always really sweet. The funny thing about what he was saying was that I'd actually been thinking about the time thing. I didn't want to be one of those women but I was definitely thinking it was time for us to have one of those "so what are we?" kind of conversations.

"I'd like that," I said. "We can make it official today. I'm your girl...not like I haven't been this whole time though."

"It's felt like he," he smiled back at me.

The rest of the week with Miles was more stuff like that. Now that we'd gotten to the point where our relationship was physical, we couldn't keep our hands off of one another. For the entire week that we were in Florida we'd spend our days on the beach, shopping, or out at a club or restaurant. At night we stayed up making love and fell asleep till late morning when we would start the cycle all over again.

By the end of the week I was more relaxed than I'd ever been. The vacation had put me into a good headspace and I just wanted to enjoy it for as long as I could. It wasn't until after we'd gotten off the plane and gotten our luggage that I realized we were back home and the vacation was over.

"So, I'm amping up the security around you," Miles said as we made our way to the airport parking lot. He'd parked there before we left and was planning on dropping me at home before he went back to his own spot.

"What does that mean?" I asked. I was wheeling my suitcase behind me.

"It means that someone is gonna be on you at all times," he said. I felt a little bad because it almost felt like the vacation was already in the past for him. He had this edge on him again. The city had made him hard all over again.

"How are you gonna do that? I don't wanna

feel like a prisoner in my own life," I said. I knew that he was trying to look out for me as best as he could but I didn't want him to take it overboard.

"It won't feel like that," he said with a shake of his head. "You're safe at the hospital. Nobody would try anything there. Your building is good but I'm just gonna have a couple more people hanging around some places."

"Fine," I said. It would be better not to argue. He'd had some of his people looking out for me before and I didn't even realize it. If it was going to be that same way then I didn't mind. "What about you though? Now that we're back here I'm worried about you, Miles."

"I'll be fine," he said. "I'll always come back to you. That's a promise. I'm not out here moving without people either."

"I just want you to be safe," I said. I was trying not to sound worried but I couldn't help it.

"I will be," he said as we got to the car. Miles opened the trunk and put both of our bags in them. He climbed into the driver's seat and I got in on my side.

The drive from their airport to my house

was about half an hour long. Miles and I were talking and listening to music as we were on our way. We'd just made another turn and were about to continue down a road when we heard sirens behind us. Miles looked into the mirror and realized they were there for us.

"What did we do?" I asked. It was no secret that cops weren't fond of people of color and from what I'd seen Miles hadn't done anything wrong so I wondered what they were stopping us for.

He pulled the car over to the side of the road. "Just be calm." He looked at me sincerely. I nodded my head.

The cop still hadn't gotten out of his car. He must've been running the tags on the car or something. Miles kept looking at the mirror to see if the cop had gotten out of the car yet.

Miles was wearing a hoodie. He reached into the pocket on the side and pulled out a large sum of cash, more cash than I'd seen in person. I didn't know when he'd grabbed the cash or if he had it with the whole time. I hadn't even seen him put it in his pockets. I knew he was paying for everything in cash in Miami though.

"Here," he said. He reached over to my lap and opened my purse, throwing the money inside. He opened his wallet and took out his ID and then put the wallet in my purse as well.

"Hold that and I'll handle this," he said.

He was right on time with his movements. The cop had gotten out of the car and so did his partner. They were walking up on both sides of the car and tapped his window when they got up to it. Miles rolled it down.

"Sir, can I have your license and registration, and your name?" the cop asked. He was white and appeared to be in his mid-30s.

"Miles Wilson," he replied as he handed the guy his license. The officer looked down at the license and asked Miles to step out of the car. Before I could say anything, he was putting the handcuffs on him. The expression on Miles' face was one of calmness. I didn't know if he knew this was going to happen, but he didn't seem to be too worried. There was concern on his face for me.

"It'll be alright," Miles said loudly.

The officers' partner tapped my window and asked me to step out of the car. I made sure my purse was closed and got out.

"What's going on? Where are you taking him?"

"Ma'am, is that your boyfriend? I'm sorry to tell you but he's under arrest. Unfortunately, we won't be able to answer any questions," he said. He reached into his pocket and pulled out a business card, handing it to me. "You or his lawyer can meet him here but he's coming with us today."

"What? How the hell can you just do this?" I asked. I wasn't crying but I was almost hysterical. Miles was being escorted to the police car.

"Do you have someone you can call to come and pick you up?" the officer asked.

"Pick me up?" I was even more confused than.

"Unfortunately, we're gonna have to take the car with us as evidence," he explained with a smirk.

"Evidence?"

He nodded his head. "That's correct. Do you have someone you can call?"

I was feeling more confused than ever. He was being nice but there was nothing but firmness in his voice which let me know that I definitely wasn't leaving in that car, or with Miles. I pulled out my phone and dialed Stella's number. I was glad when she picked up and even more glad when she said she wasn't at work. I asked her to come and get me, letting her know that I'd explain everything when I saw her.

"I just don't know what to do," I said with tears streaming down my face. Stella had come to pick me up soon after I called. She'd asked a lot of questions but I told her that she'd get the full story once I was back in the house.

We'd gone to my apartment and she listened while I explained everything to her. She tried to ask questions but I told her it would just be easier for me to tell her the whole story once.

"Kallie, did you know he had the money in the car?" Stella asked. She had a serious look on her face. I knew she was judging me for being with Miles. "If you did, it's alright. They didn't search you or anything."

I shook my head. "No, Stella," I said. "Like I told you, he paid for everything cash, but I didn't know he was walking around with all that money."

After we were safely away from the police, I looked at all the money that Miles had stuff into it. I realized then that it was packed together in rubber bands but from the looks of it there had to be almost $300,000.

"I'm sorry for asking. This is all just a lot for me to take in. You didn't even tell me you two were dating," she said. "And you said they didn't tell you what they were taking him for?"

"No," I said. "I called the number on the card that the cop gave me but they said they have no record of miles or anything with his name."

"Kallie, what aren't you telling me?" Stella asked. I was glad that she had come and picked me up but my patience was wearing thin for her. She had so many questions and I didn't have answers for her. "Why would they take Miles? What is it that he does for a living?"

"You already know the answer to that," I said to her as I looked her in the eyes. She' been the one telling me this entire time about Miles and how he had to be involved in some bad stuff. Two plus two made four. I was sure it was obvious to her.

Stella shook her head. "Look, you know I'm all for taking a walk on the wild side. I think everyone should try and live their best life, but I don't want you to be dumb about things. You're way too smart to think that this has a happy ending."

"Stella, I know you're trying to help, but this isn't the time for this. I don't know where Miles is or who to contact to try and find out and you're telling me to just leave him alone?" I couldn't believe she was taking this chance to try and drive her point home.

"It's the best time to talk about it. It's still fresh in your mind," Stella said. I didn't know if she was trying to kick me when I was down but it was working. I opened my mouth to really give her a piece of my mind but luckily for her, my cell phone vibrated with a text message.

Open the door, the text read. I didn't recognize the number but it was a Chicago one. Right after that there was a knock at the door. I looked at Stella cautiously and then got up to answer it.

The man standing on the other side of the door was familiar. He was there the night my would-be attacker was stabbed. He worked for, or with, Miles.

"I need that thing that Miles gave you," he said. He had a serious look on his face. Recognition crossed mine as I let the door close. I headed towards the kitchen and grabbed a plastic bag. I emptied the money and the wallet into it and then headed back to the door, handing it to the guy.

"So, what next?" I asked, nervous about what was to come.

FIND out what happens next in part two of Enticed By A Kingpin! Available Now!

To FIND out when Mia Black has new books available, **follow Mia Black on Instagram: @authormiablack**

ENTICED BY A KINGPIN 2

Kallie never imagined she'd find herself drawn to a man like Miles, but something about him keeps pulling her closer. A relationship could complicate her life and her career.

Christian is used to getting what he wants, but Kallie's budding relationship with Miles is getting in his way. Unaccustomed to rejection, Christian will stop at nothing to ensure he doesn't lose – even if that means he'll have to ruin Kallie's career to win.

Two men, both dangerous, want Kallie, but is she willing to let either of them stake a claim on her?

Find out what happens in part two of Enticed By A Kingpin!

To find out when Mia Black has new books available, **follow Mia Black on Instagram: @authormiablack**

CPSIA information can be obtained
at www.ICGtesting.com
Printed in the USA
LVHW081308190220
647479LV00017B/544